Wait long enough and death will find you. It didn't care what religion you were or your race or even how much money you made. Death was a certain guarantee.

The BIG question was the when.

Death is Born

From the time she was very young, she knew that she was different from everyone else. Not physically, but mentally. For her this was just a fact that she accepted as she grew into womanhood. When she was eight years old she had watched as her grandparents passed away one by one and then one of her friends at the ripe old age of 7 died in a car accident with her parents.

She watched as everyone cried and the sadness in their eyes, but she was indifferent. She felt neither sorrow nor joy. She just knew that death could find you anywhere. It really didn't occur to her till she was 10 that death could be controlled. It happened a week after her parents took her to the state fair and she won a goldfish which and after a week of forgetting to feed or give it fresh water, died.

Finding the goldfish belly up would have made any other kid at least some-what sad, but she felt nothing. Looking back now she knew that this was the beginning of her true calling. Trying out her new found control of death she began practicing on larger life sustaining creatures. The next being a turtle, then a hamster and finally a stray cat that she placed inside a clear plastic garbage bag and watched as it died. To say that she enjoyed killing things would in her mind be wrong. She didn't feel the rush of watching death overtake a living creature nor was she sad. She was, if anything, feeling a sense of control. She knew that she had the power to take life when it suited her.

Chapter One: Three Years Before

"Damn, I am never drinking again," Ryan Thompson said to himself for the 100th time that day. He thought back to last night and the beers and shots of Jack Daniels he and his wife had consumed till the wee hours of the morning. What a night. The alcohol alone would have made a young man swear off drinking, then you add in the wild sex and what you had was a man in his 50's feeling like he should be shot to be put out of his misery. The thought of completing this roof repair job and then home to bed was all that was keeping him going. No sex and definitely no alcohol tonight.. He had thought about calling in sick that day but as the foreman of a roofing company it didn't look good calling in the day after

July 4th. He'd fired guys for doing that. It was all he could do to keep going through the day and when the call came in from the main office saying someone had just called and said the tile roofing near the chimney on the Wayman's house were cracked. Ryan jumped on the chance. It was on his way home and the sooner he saw the back of his eyelids the better. Before leaving the job he was on he called his wife to say he'd be coming home early and that he was giving up drinking. They both laughed at that statement.

Arriving he removed the extension ladder from the back of his pick-up truck and was wondering how the hell could roof tiles already be cracked on a roof he and his crew had just finished installing three months ago. Setting the extension ladder up in the back of the house where there were no new shrubs or expensive vegetation to trample on, he walked back to his truck to grab a caulk gun and a rag. He'd fix it temporarily today and come back Monday and do the job right. Today was all about quick and easy. Sitting the extension ladder up 30 feet would be no easy task for any man but Ryan had been setting up and climbing ladders his whole life. Everyone joked that he was part bionic squirrel. Grabbing the caulk gun and placing it and 2 tubes of caulk in a 5 gallon bucket and stuffing the rags in his back jean's pocket Ryan insured the ladder was stabilized and on good footing before climbing the 26 feet to the top. The roof was dry today and all Ryan could hope for now was for the chance to throw some

caulk on those tiles before the sky opened up. It was coming and the sky was getting dark…His luck held. Almost.

He threw some quick drying caulk on the tiles haphazardly and was rushing to reach the ladder when the rain started. "Shit! Damn rain couldn't have waited 5 more minutes!" Ryan was thinking. The rain, though a hindrance, didn't faze him that much. He was a Florida Cracker and a little rain never would stop a roofer. As he reached the top of the ladder he looked down out of habit to ensure the ladder was still stabilized. As he climbed down his thoughts turned again to how in less than 30 minutes he would be home getting ready to climb into a nice soft bed. No shower tonight, just that bed! In that next instant Ryan's thoughts turned in another direction. The ladder for some reason was beginning to tilt to the right. Trying to use his body to counter weight the ladder tilt he was surprised when it continued to fall. Looking for anything to grab and finding nothing, he continued his downward fall. Shit! Shit! Shit! Was all he could think to yell as he fell the 22 feet onto the concrete. Hitting the concrete hard Ryan lost consciousness for a few seconds and came to as the wind slowly returned to his lungs. Damn that was close he thought. As he tried to rise he realized part of his body wasn't responding. Then came the pain. Not just pain, but a lot of blood screaming pain. Ryan found that his entire right side was broken or so it felt. Shit! Just when he thought luck was beginning to turn his way, this happened. As he laid back Ryan realized he had left his cell phone in the truck. He was about to contemplate trying to make it to his trucks when he saw someone approaching him

Hell yes! Now to the hospital, fix me up and back to my comfortable life was one of the last thoughts he was to have. Ryan was surprised when the person walked over to him consoling him with talk of helping him, lifted his head up a few feet as if to help him.

The very last thought to enter Ryan's mind was why the fuck would this person lift my head up so far and why are they pushing it down so hard and fast onto the concrete?

Chapter 2

Maggie Depew's nickname behind her back was 'Mama Smurf '. She stood a little over five feet tall and had a slightly larger than normal nose and dark blond hair which nowadays came out of a bottle. Single all her life, Maggie was married to her job in a sense. Not that she didn't socialize or date, she just had never met anyone that she found that intelligent or 'cute' to her standards. At 58 she had been with Harvest Salt Insurance company for 40 years and had started as a receptionist right out of high school with the company when everyone who worked for the company could fit into the break room for the Christmas party. Now with over 200 employees she was lucky to remember everyone's name. She had worked her way up the ladder taking night classes and now she was lead investigator for one of the biggest insurance companies in the States. Maggie and her team didn't handle the day to day pay out of $250,000 or less. No, this team was made for the power player insurance policies. When a pay-out for a Ryan Smith insurance policy crossed her desk for a $450,000 accidental death policy Maggie was not surprised or even intrigued. The police and coroner had both signed documentation stating that Ryan Smith's death from falling from a ladder was accidental. Maggie knew that the police and most coroners were right 99% of the time. It was that 1% that Harvest Salt paid her and her team for.

Knowing that she had one team member on vacation, one on maternity leave and one investigating a case in California it would fall upon her to fly to Florida to check out the facts.

Maggie flew out of Delaware the next morning heading for Tampa, Florida. After renting a car and checking in to her motel room she set up appointments with the police who handled the case, the coroner who saw the body and lastly the widow, a Julie Thompson who was also the beneficiary. Maggie's meeting with the police went exactly as it had in any other state and she had met police and coroners from most of them. The police with their clean cut uniforms that looked tailor made for them, said

what she had heard over a 100 times before, "No sign of foul play", "No signs of violence", "No evidence to suggest anything other than it being an accident." Thanking them she headed to her next appointment with the coroner.

Arriving, Maggie was greeted by an elderly gentleman who introduced himself as Dr. Schipero. Maggie and the Doc could have been brother and sister; they resembled each other so closely with the short stature and age. Maggie was betting he was called 'Papa

Smurf' behind his back. Doc Schipero was not one to mince words and said directly to Maggie that though it was a pleasure to meet her, he was pretty sure she made the trip for nothing.

Maggie played the game. "Doctor, it said in the death report that Mr. Thompson died from head trauma when he hit the concrete. What other injuries did he have?"

Doctor Schipero said without a pause, "Mr. Thompson's autopsy revealed multiple broken bones on his right side which, though serious, were not enough to kill him. His blood test revealed some slight alcohol content but nothing else. No narcotics. I attributed the alcohol to the day of his death being July 5th and I'm betting Mr. Thompson, like most Americans, probably tied one on the night before. What killed Mr. Thompson was his head injury. By the looks of his skull and brain he died almost instantly. Maggie knew she was wasting her time if the coroner said that death was caused by a head injury.

"Doctor Schipero, let me ask you one last question, off the record if that's agreeable?"

The doctor actually gave a slight smile. Maggie had noticed that Doctor Schipero was not wearing a wedding ring and was kinda cute in his own way. Seemed intelligent too. Smiling back, Maggie said,"Let me ask you first, you and I have been through countless reports and we both know that the coroner may notice things that don't have a spot on that report form. What was your impression of Mr. Thompson's body other than the obvious?"

For once Dr. Schipero didn't answer quickly. "Off the record you said?"

"Of course. It goes no further than here."

"The first thing I noticed about Mr. Smith was his smell of alcohol. He smelt like a wino who had alcohol pouring out of his cells. It was strong enough to override the smell of his blood. I expected a high reading on his blood alcohol reading but he came back very low telling me this guy was a big drinker. Not a couple of beers guy but someone who consumed a large amount of alcohol daily and as he sweated he was bringing the alcohol with it. I stated that Mr. Thomson had a slight alcohol reading, but this smell was from a heavy drinker." Doc Schipero took a moment and continued, "What else was strange was that Mr. Thompson was 52 years old but looking at the body I had to check the records. This man looked to be in his seventies. Now the Florida sun will age a man who works in it all day long but this guy had been rode hard. I'm betting he was very familiar with the bottom of a bottle."

Maggie made a mental note and said, "I said just one question but I do have one more. How did Mrs. Thompson act when you talked to her?"

Again, without hesitation the doctor replied, "She acted like I expected her to. She was honestly upset. If I had to say anything it was I believe that was one woman who honestly loved her husband. I was taken aback by the age difference, but she definitely loved her husband."

Maggie then gave the doctor her best smile.

"Thanks Doctor. I have to meet with Ms. Thompson in 45 minutes but I am staying at the Hampton Inn if you think of anything else." Maggie continued smiling looking the doctor directly in the eyes as she passed him her business card. Hell, even old ladies can flirt, she thought to herself.

Maggie met with Julie Thompson who showed all the signs of a grieving widow. After the initial shock about seeing how young she looked she answered every question as any one who was devastated by the death of a husband would. Mrs. Thompson's mother was with her in her time of need and held Julie as she spoke to Maggie. Doctor Shapiro was right. This woman loved her now deceased husband. When Maggie returned to

Delaware three days later, she signed the necessary paperwork stating that Mr. Ryan Thompson's death was accidental and ensured the $450,000 was processed. It also turns out that Doctor Schipiro did have some additional information to tell Maggie when he contacted her at the Hampton Inn that night. It wasn't anything involving the case. But to Maggie it was far more interesting. She had spent the next two days with him.

Her early teen years were an adventure not just in puberty, which she considered (with her period and pimples) a royal pain in the ass .
No, what she enjoyed more than anything was planning death and the rewards it could bring. She didn't enjoy killing nor did she hate it. To be honest if asked at this time she would have just said that she had no feeling either way. Live , die, it made no difference. What she wanted more than anything was the reward at the end of the tunnel.
What she didn't realize at this time is that she was slowly growing into a psychopath.

Chapter Three – 15 years before.

 One usually comes to the Florida beaches to enjoy the sun and sea and to pretend there's another life out there waiting for them.. For one couple, Brandon and Tracy Elbit, the drive to get away and relax over a long weekend would be a life changing event. Upon arriving at their motel in Pass-A-Grill Florida that they would call home for the next four days, the couple unpacked and started the clock on the fun and frolic awaiting them. Packing hastily the usual fare of suntan lotion, beach towels and the additional toys and necessities needed to spend an afternoon on the beach, Brandon and Tracy were in the grips of bliss knowing that the fun was only starting. The sun was almost at its peak and was so hot it almost took their breath away as they walked towards the beach. Throwing a

couple of towels down in the sand and dropping their beach necessities, the two didn't bother to stop to apply sunscreen. The water looked that inviting. Holding hands like two new lovers they stepped into the surf. The waves bathed them in a cool refreshing liquid. Smiling like a couple of high school sweethearts they continued to walk out towards the deeper water. A few feet out and Brandon thought that he walked on a dead dolphin or some other large type of dead sea creature. He waited for the waves to recede and peered down to realize that the sea creature resembled the torso of a human. Tracy who had paused to wait for Brandon to continue was peering down also when the sea water became clear enough for them to see that in fact a man was peering up, eyes wide open and with a couple of crabs hanging from his body. A great beginning to a vacation the man was thinking as his wife threw up.

Knowing right from wrong is something you're taught from the time you are born. She learned that early in life. You're schooled that killing a fellow human being is wrong and if you do kill someone there will be severe consequences. The thought of being locked away for years scared the hell out of her. Looking up the accidental death rates she found that over 100,000 thousand people died yearly from accidents. She thought to herself that more than a few of them had to be murder. Also she read that women used poison as their number one murder weapon. What idiots. No, her accidental deaths would be never proven and she sure the hell wasn't using poison.

Chapter 4 – Present Day

Maggie was still employed by the Harvest Salt Insurance Company when her friend and employer, Micheal Wood, asked her to meet him for lunch at a local restaurant. Arriving 10 minutes early she was surprised to see not

only Micheal but Raymond Gante, a gentleman she knew was the owner of a competitive Insurance company located not far from the Harvest Salt Insurance building here in Wilmington, Delaware. Trying not to appear surprised Maggie was introduced to Raymond Gante and shaking his hand knew that something important was happening. A few minutes of small talk and ordering coffee all around, Micheal got to the point. "Maggie, Raymond and I asked you here to talk to you about a case you handled three years ago. A man by the name of Ryan Thompson died from an accidental death. You remember the case?" Maggie, who never forgot a case, remembered it like it was yesterday. Plus that's when she had met Doctor Jimmy Schipero. Saying she did, Mr. Wood continued.

"Well it seems as if the widow, Julie, went ahead and got herself married again almost two years ago, And lo and behold this one just died from an accidental death one week ago." Maggie was taking all this in, trying to figure out the probability of two husbands dying accidental deaths less than three years apart. The numbers were very high. Raymond

Gant, who had said very little til then asked, "Maggie, was there anything you found unusual about Julie or anything about this case?"

Taking her time before answering she said, "Not really. I wish I could tell you that the widow seemed happy or that she seemed nervous or the coroner found PCP in the deceased husband's blood. But nothing like that even showed a hint of popping up. This was one of the easiest accidental deaths I could have signed off on. Hell even OSHA was there and said it was accidental. They said that Ryan didn't follow the correct procedures for stabilizing and wearing a harness"

"So nothing gave you a doubt?" Raymond continued. Maggie thought back to that 1% that bothered Doctor Shapiro about the case. "I didn't say

that. What I'm saying is that this was one of the easiest accidental death case's I've ever handled. Now as far as a doubt, yes, I had a small percentage that I attributed to it being too easy. I've handled or been involved with over a hundred of these accidental deaths cases and for some reason it felt different. Almost too perfect. It's very hard to explain." Maggie didn't mention that Dr. Schipero was the one who had put that doubt into Maggie's head.

Raymond smiled at her and said, "Maggie, mostly everyone thinks I'm a heartless SOB, but years ago I too worked myself up from an insurance salesman to claims and investigations, then to starting my own company. I do know that feeling. Now our Miss Julie just put in for a $750,000 claim to be paid for accidental death for her latest husband. So between Micheal and I she's going to walk away with over a million dollars. For that kind of money we both agreed to work together to see whether something was not right in Dodge. That's where you come in. Micheal said you were the best so we'd like you to go to Florida tomorrow and meet with a private Investigation firm called S and W. They'll be working for you and we want you to take a look at this last accident and maybe take a look at the first one again. Interested?"

"S and W? Never heard of them." Maggie knew all the major detective firms and S and W"s name had never come up before.

" Almost no one has. And apparently that's the way they like it. But we asked around and heard they were the best but very expensive. And they're local to that area so that should make it easier. And with the percentage they're going to take if we don't have to pay out, they are not cheap. Also you should know up front that we were told they were nothing like they appear and the word unorthodox kept popping up. Mostly with a grin as they said it from the few people who knew of them. We were told that if we wanted to know what was going on, the money we would have to pay was worth it."

"You say Julie's second husband died in an accident? What were the circumstances in this one?

"Well husband number two went and blew himself up in his workshop. Apparently, he was welding and gas built up and took out everything. Luckily the workshop was located far enough away from the house that it wasn't touched. Damn house is insured for another

$750.000. We went ahead and sent everything we had over to S and W yesterday once we signed our life away. They can explain everything to you to save time. So Maggie, feel like another trip to sunny Florida.?"

Maggie, with little hesitation said "Yes" and went home to pack her carry-on for a few days stay in beautiful Florida. She called her Doctor Jimmy Schipero and told him she was coming. He was delighted but for some reason she felt he knew already. Looking forward to seeing Jimmy she kept thinking what had the two insurance agency CEO's meant by unorthodox?'.

Knowing that the most important quality she would need would be patience. She knew with practice she could achieve patience. She watched as people became pissed off as they waited in line for such trivial crap at any convenient store. She watched as one guy became so irate that he had threatened to call the Manager and was cussing and acting like a fool all because he wasn't being taken care of immediately. Where the hell was he going that life was dependent on his extra 5 minutes of time that was so important? No, he could never do what she planned to do. She just waited in line in her own little world, running through the perfect murder's time and time again. Learning to control her breathing and let nothing affect her thinking she knew she was almost there. Hell, she even went to Barnes and Nobles and bought books on learning patience.

Chapter 5

The arrival time at Tampa was 9:10 am. Maggie's initial plan was to land, rent a car, check into her motel then drive to S and W. Late last night her boss called and said S and W had different plans and that someone would meet her at the airport. Forget the motel also. Upon landing she was looking for that guy that's always standing there with your name on a piece of white cardboard. When a beautiful lady who looked to be in her late 50's came up to her and said she was from S and W and her name was Rita and that she was here to pick her up AND they had to hurry because Michelle was driving. As they walked, Rita called someone and said they were exiting now. As they waited at the arrival sidewalk Maggie was even more surprised when a younger, good looking, blond woman pulled up in a 12 passenger van with blacked out windows. She promptly hopped out and introduced herself as Michelle as she gave Maggie a hug. Not a handshake but a hug.

Following Rita, she walked to the back of the van placing her overnight bag inside wondering what exactly she had gotten herself into. Not sure where she was supposed to sit or what door to open, Rita said to the younger one named Michelle that she was driving and to sit in the passenger seat and opened the sliding doors for Maggie to sit. Inside were two beautiful ladies that appeared very happy to have Rita driving by their conversation regarding the driving by Michelle. One of the ladies moved back a row giving Maggie space to sit next to a baby sleeping soundly in a car carrier that doubled as a bassinet. Maggie, who could keep her composure through just about anything said to the driver, Rita, "Excuse me, I'm supposed to meet with the detectives at S and W and was wondering how long it would take before we reached their office."

Rita just smiled as did the rest of the ladies before saying, "Maggie, relax, were all partners of S and W, except for Lil Sammy there sleeping besides you who's got a few more years. Michelle, myself and you are going to interview Julia, the deceased husband's wife at three this afternoon so that leaves us plenty of time to do some shopping and have

lunch on the beach. Those two ladies behind you will be joining us. Now let me concentrate and get us out of this traffic."

Looking in the rear view mirror Rita said, "Ladies, introduce yourself and tell me exactly how bad Michelle's driving was. "

 Maggie was confused. Expecting this to be a business meeting she had dressed in a professional business suit and had planned on reviewing the case with the detectives as soon as she landed in Tampa. She was just beginning to glimpse what unorthodox meant. But maybe unorthodox might not quite be the word she would use. Rita could see her confusion in Maggie's face in the rear mirror. "Hey Maggie, don't worry. Things are in progress that you'll see shortly. Now just sit back and relax and we'll get some clothes that suit you better for Florida."

Thinking back she knew 17 years ago that she had tried, no, not tried, she had wished with all her heart that she could be like other kids. She knew as hard as she pretended that deep inside her, she was not even close.

The first boy she had dated came so close to dying that even today it scared her when she thought about it. With no planning it would have been instantaneous, like a reflex. She learned that night the true meaning of patience.

His name was Richard or as everyone called him, Rich. He was tall, had a nice head of hair which he wore in a ponytail and was the tall silent type. She had hoped he was the one that she could relate to. He paid for the movie and held her hand which she thought might be a little too forward. She had no idea of his thoughts about life. But having read enough books and watched enough movies she knew that was normal. She couldn't understand why. This dickhead doesn't even know me. She played the game.

On the way home as he was taking her home she tried to ask a couple of questions to feel him out. All he wanted to do was talk about himself. What a dumbass.

Dropping her off he had actually tried touching her breast and had tried to go lower. He had slid his penis out of his pants and she's thinking to herself that he has nothing to offer her except his own self satisfaction.

Right there and then she knew she could kill him. Slide the knife out of her purse, cut his throat and watch as he bled out.

Instead she looked at his penis and told him, "If that's the best you got then you get the hell out of here and call me when that little thing grows." Laughing at him as she exited, she watched as he threw his car into reverse and peeled off down the road.

Three important lessons were learnt that night:

1) People, especially men, can be intimidated.

2) Men were pigs and only interested in one thing.

3) She was not ready. She had to learn better patience.

Chapter 6

Sam and JR weren't happy. They had left Tampa at 9 am that morning and drove to Dr. Roberts house in St. Petersburg where the first accidental death occurred three years ago. Both of them hated 'accidental death cases'. Murder they loved, screwing the government culprits, sure. But most of the time with accidental deaths it was almost 100 percent accidental death. Then if it wasn't you had at least some clue. This one had OSHA, State and local police and other government agencies saying the cause of death was accidental. Knocking on the Roberts front door they weren't surprised when no one answered. These were wealthy snowbirds and with the weather being hotter than a bitch, the Robert's were most likely relaxing somewhere the weather was cooler.

Walking to the back of the Roberts house they kept looking at the roof. Using the diagrams that had been sent to them by Harvest Salt Insurance the two went to where the ladder had made its fatal fall. The two men never said a word to each other but just looked around imagining in their minds that fateful afternoon when Ryan fell to his death.

"Damn Sam, that's a hell of a way up there. I don't think I'd have the balls to go up there alone without a spotter."

"You and I both. JR, this side walk is three feet wide at least. I'm wondering why Ryan would place it so close to the edge to allow it to slip off into the dirt?" JR was wondering the same thing. But accidents do happen.

"Sam, let's say someone did want Ryan dead. What would be the chances of someone following him from work, then sneaking behind him while he's up on the roof and rearranging the ladder so it falls? There's no guarantee he would die. He may have just broken an arm or leg. I'm not seeing it."

Sam was deep in thought. After a few minutes he said, "All right, let's look at this from another perspective. What happens if we change the scenario to knowing that the killer was already here?"

"How the hell would the killer know that the tiles were going to be busted on the roof and that Ryan would be the one to come out and fix it? Come on Sam, you're grasping at straws here."

Sam looked at JR smiling. "Remember the day he died you idiot? It was July 5th." A circuit in JR's brain finally connected.

"No shit. Yeah, then it's possible. Still very far-fetched but possible."

The two discussed what 'could have happened' if someone really wanted Ryan dead for the next 15 minutes. The question now was how to prove an accident wasn't an accident with little or nothing to go on. With the time now almost 10 am the two decided that no other usefulness could come from them standing there and decided that fishing off Sam's boat should take priority. It would give them time to think. Or at least that's the story they would tell.

Maggie was having the time of her life. The morning and afternoon had gone perfectly. The ladies from S and W were as nice and genuine as any of her friends in Delaware. It was as if she had known them forever. The baby, Lil Sam, was as cute as could be and only cried once when he was hungry. She was very surprised when she asked what the ladies did at S and W and
was told nicely that they were partners and did everything that needed to be done. Rita saw the confusion on Maggie's face for the umpteenth time that day. Smiling, Rita explained that everyone who worked at S and W were partners after they had completed a probationary period if one was needed.

"Everyone works hard and makes the same amount in their paycheck as the next person. S and W was started years ago and ever since then it has been the same. No one has to brown nose or kiss ass to anyone. All of our concentration and effort goes into the case's were assigned."

"Then who's in charge? Who are the detectives?"

Smiling, Rita answered, "Honey we all are. We have an office administrator, Phil, who assigns the cases and is married to Barbara, who's sitting behind you, who happens to be our financial manager and best of all we have JR and Michelle for the tough cases. These two are the brains of our operation. I'd include Sam, my better half but he's semi-retired. Or so he says. We also have an additional eight other detectives.

Maggie, who had a hundred more questions, remained silent and just enjoyed a peaceful, fun filled afternoon with her new friends. As the afternoon of shopping and lunch came to an end and they were making their way to the interview with Julia, Rita received a phone call on the car phone. Maggie was told to not say a word. Rita had an ear to ear grin on her face and said, "This should be good."

Pushing the answer button on the steering wheel she said, "Hi Sweetie".

An older man's voice, who Maggie would learn shortly was Sam, Rita's husband, replied, "Hi Hon. Hey JR and I need you guys to do us a favor."

"I'm listening."

"We'd like for you and Michelle to go in first and start the interview and just ask some casual questions . Then have Maggie come in 5 minutes later and ask her a couple of questions. You want to have someone write these down?"

"Not necessary, I have you on speaker so Michelle is listening." Maggie wondered what Michelle had to do with not writing it down.

"Great. Hi guys. JR and I have been working our butts off. We have a couple of great theories for you." All the S and W ladies in the Van tried to

keep from laughing out loud. "So anyway we'd really like Maggie to ask first when she goes in, first, what happened to the ladder that Ryan was using at the Waymens. Was it sold? Was it the companies? How can she find out? Push that question. Second, ask Julia if she knows what ever became of the tiles he was fixing? Did his company go back out and change them or fix them? Next we want Maggie to ask nonchalantly as you three are leaving, did Ryan have any enemies. Give her time to think about it. And lastly, we want to make sure Maggie that you give her your business card and say that if you think of anything we'd love to know. I'm thinking just stick to Ryan's accidental death and let Julia and her mother know you'll be coming back soon to discuss the last husband's death tomorrow. Don't ask about the second husband's death at all this time, just stick with Ryan's death."

"Sam, you think it could have been a staged accident?" Rita pretty much knew that answer before she asked it.

"It's possible. But whoever planned it thought of everything. Michelle, are you all set on your end?"

"Yes. We're going to do a sound check with Tim in just a few minutes."

"Great. How's Lil Sam doing? Does he miss me?"

"Oh yeah. He hasn't stopped crying since he has seen you."

"That's my boy. Okay we'll see you for dinner. Oh and I forgot. Hey Maggie, we had a couple of questions for Dr. Schipero so we invited him for dinner tonight to go over Ryan's autopsy. I believe you two know each other? Okay guys were off to brainstorm. Love you babe."

"Love you too. See you in an hour or so. Don't work too hard." Disconnected, all the ladies burst into laughter. Maggie, who had no idea where the joke lay just stared at everyone. Michelle turned around and told Maggie that a GPS tracker had been installed in Sam's phone and they knew those two had been fishing since 10:30 this morning.

Who the hell were these people? And what had the gentleman Sam been referring to when he said he thought Dr. Shipero and she knew each other. Did he say that with a little bit of sarcasm in his voice?

Before arriving at the interview Rita pulled over at a local gas station where Michelle removed a purse from under the passenger seat. Looking inside she took out a small earpiece which she inserted into her right ear. Next a miniature microphone was inserted inside her blouse collar. "You there Tim?" she asked in a normal tone of voice. "Test, 1,2,3 Peter Piper picked a peck of pickled Peppers." The same testing was repeated for the additional two listening devices. Once testing of the equipment was complete Michelle looked over at Rita and said seriously "Let's get this over with. I'm getting hungry again."

The interview with Julia and her mom lasted for less than 20 minutes and the ladies made it back to home base, which turned out to be JR's and Michelle's home or as Maggie saw it, mansion by 4:30. No discussion of the conversation was discussed on the way home. It seemed as if Rita and Michelle were thinking long and hard about what transpired. Maggie, who had done numerous interviews, thought everything went perfectly and had asked her question according to plan.

Maggie was totally unprepared for home base. She had been in big houses before, but this one was different. It looked like a small mansion located by the inter coastal water way. Once inside she tried to take everything in at once. At first she was greeted by two of the ugliest dogs she had seen. The one they called Venus was more interested in making sure Lil Sam was in one piece then sniffing her. The other one, who she found out was called GD Dog, gave her a sniff and went back to the kitchen, which she later found out had a built-in doggie door which went out to the lanai and pool. Rita gave her a very quick tour and then showed her to one of the 6 guest rooms located on the right side of the house upstairs, each with its own bathroom, the left side of the house was Michelle's and JR's domain she was told. Rita told her to relax for a few, then come on down for drinks by the pool. Maggie was curious why no one had asked her about Dr. Shapiro since she was assuming everyone knew.

After a quick rinse me off shower she found that making her way outside was no easy task. Going downstairs Maggie passed a billiards room, a big

office with 4 computers and copiers of every sort where she saw a younger lady working on a computer whose hands were flying across a keyboard who never looked up. She had thought of asking the lady how the hell did she get to the lanai but this lady was so deep into her work she decided she could figure this out on her own. (plus she had her pride.) She passed a huge dining room, a game room, a family room then she finally finally saw the huge kitchen that looked like an upscale restaurant kitchen , that's when she remembered it led to the lanai. Reaching the sliding glass doors that led to the lanai she realized as she had walked through the house (or mansion) it struck her that it was not by the vastness or money it must have cost but the simplicity and hominess the aura of the place gave out. From the outside most people would expect to find sculptures or fancy paintings with modern or expensive furniture you were afraid to sit in.

Not here. Decorated in Florida style you felt like you may be in a typical Floridian beach home. Some rooms had the old clapboard ceilings with walls painted in soft pastels with sea pictures of beaches, ships and sunsets of all types. Pictures of JR and Michelle on different beaches or with Sam and Rita filled one wall in the dining room. Another was Lil Sam and GD dog and Venus. Walking through the sliding glass doors to the outside she found herself walking into a two story screened in lanai with a huge Olympic size pool with a waterfall , surrounded by tables and chairs that made her think of an all inclusive resort in the Caribbean. Soft tropical music was playing in speakers she couldn't see. Off to the far right was what she was betting was the jacuzzi and shower rooms. Dressed in her new shorts and top which the ladies had helped her pick out and having taken a quick shower and doing her hair she still felt inadequate compared to all these beautiful people surrounding her. She felt like a donkey at a horse show. That feeling left her when a tall older gentleman wearing a gold hoop earring with long gray hair in a ponytail yelled across the pool deck, "Hey JR, the new maids here. Have her get me a couple of six packs out of the frig and put them in the cooler."

Maggie just stood there looking stupid for a split second. Seeing Rita seated in the shade under a palm tree with Lil Sam in her lap smiling looking at her, Maggie yelled to her, " Hey Rita, you said all your people were great detectives. Where'd you get this asshole?"

That was all it took. Genuine laughter could be heard from everyone. To make it even more perfect her Jimmy, aka: Dr. Schipero was here and got out of the pool and gave her a hug and whispered, "Damn I missed you!" Maggie blushed the color of deep red reserved for school girls getting their first kiss. Sam of course who was watching couldn't resist. "Go ahead Maggster, give Dr. D. a big kiss!" Maggie did while she also extended her middle finger towards Sam. Maggie didn't know it but she was becoming a part of the S and W family. After Maggie was handed her favorite drink without asking by Sam who was chief bartender and grill master, and things were settling down, Sam gave the announcement in a drill sergeant's voice, "Stop dicking around and earn our paychecks! Meeting starts 5 minutes before we eat."

Maggie realized then as everyone became serious that fun time was over and that the people around her were professionals. Maggie watched with her Jimmy by her side as everyone got out of the pool and semi dried off and grabbed a chair and moved it close to the barbecue grill where Sam was standing. Michelle's husband who she was introduced to as JR had moved his chair also and stood up from the chair he had been sitting in next to Michelle in the shade said, "Sam, the friggin smokes blowing into some people's eyes." Shaking his head in disbelief JR said, "New plan. AWAY from the grill. Rita, has he had his meds today?"

"JR, your hamburger has a little something in it. Enjoy!" Sam was smiling. Once everyone was settled in the new location, away from the grill, JR started. "Ok, it's really nice to see everyone here. Phil, when was the last time we had almost all the partners together?

"Let's see, that would be 8 months ago, when Lil Sam was born."

"Damn, Time is flying!. Anyway we're going to talk later about something that's on everyone's mind, but for now we're going to talk about the accidental death cases were involved with. You all have met Dr.

Schipero and Maggie, so I'm going to give you the facts, what little they are, then hear from Dr. Schipero than Michelle, Rita and Maggie and get your best Einstein's opinion."

"So today Sam and I went to the Wayman's home where the first accident occured and using Sam's great deduction skills we realized that the ladder could have been moved while the deceased was on the roof, but, I'm saying now it could have been moved and again another big could have, but it would almost take someone with a lot of balls to do it and hope he or she wasn't seen by anyone including Ryan. And to insure the ladder fell with Ryan Thompson on it would take a little ingenuity. So the bottom line is that it could have been murder. Now there are a number of scenarios that we could play out on how it was done, but we won't know since we can't prove anything. If this was intentional, then who or whomever did this is smart. Real smart. Michelle smart." Michelle, who had Lil Sam on her lap just smiled.

"My biggest issue was how did the killer or killers know that the Roberts, the owners of the house who were up north at the time, would have busted tile on their roof? And believe it or not it was Sam who figured this one out. We know that taking a ladder and setting it up to go up on a roof might be noticed plus it takes a hell of a man to set up a 30 foot ladder, then climb it and use a hammer to break a couple of tiles then climb back down and then remove the ladder. The chances of someone doing that is just too great of a chance.

Yesterday Sam reminded me that it was July 5th when the call came in about busted tiles. Say you wanted to bust someone's roof tile? What would be the easiest way without a ladder? Remember it was 3 stories high." JR waited a few seconds before answering.

"A rifle, pellet gun, or even a slingshot. Think about it.." He waited for it to sink in as he passed out aerial photos to everyone.

"I asked Tina to pull up an aerial view of the Wayman's house and include the houses that were behind it. Now from the ground all we could

see were trees keeping the house semi hidden. Now if you look closely at the surrounding houses I'm 99 percent sure one of these two houses I have circled would be able to see the Wayman's roof from a top story window. So now we know that the tiles could be broken easily if you had access to any of these homes. And I'm also 99 percent sure that someone knew that this house was under warranty with Ryan's company and since it was very close to his house on a day after heavy drinking, he would jump on the chance to fix it and be home early."

Someone asked JR if he thought they would be able to prove this scenario and open it up as a murder case. JR looked at everyone and smiled, "There's not a chance in hell. Oh were going thru with investigating it as a murder but were most likely wasting our time. No I think whoever masterminded this accident, again I'm not sure it wasn't an accident, then they thought of everything. We'd never bring this to court without something a lot more substantial."

"And how do we accomplish this?" Maggie asked without realizing she had spoken out loud.

JR was looking at Maggie smiling, "You, Rita and Michelle interviewed Julia today and a plan was started in motion to find out if it's worth proceeding. Tomorrow begins phase two which we'll talk about in a few minutes after we hear first from Doctor D and see what he thinks, then let's have the ladies tell us about the interview with Julia after Michelle gives us a run down on the family. Remember we are not thinking about the last husband's accident now. Lets deal only with only Ryans and then we'll discuss husband number two soon. First though let's hear from Doctor D."

Maggie whispered to her Jimmy, "Dr. D?"

" Yeah. It stands for Doctor Death. Sam started it and it caught on."

Sam who still stood behind the barbecue grill spoke to everyone," And we're going to keep this short cause I got some medium rare steaks that will soon be turning into well done."

Doctor Shapiro gave his official and unofficial report of examining Ryan Thompson to the group. When he finished Rita asked him how he found Julia's and her mothers behavior at that time.

"Julia was the model of a woman whose husband just died. I've seen plenty of bereaved spouses in my time and she acted as expected. Now for the Mom, it was the same. She never left her side, literally. It was as if she had to hold her up, which is not uncommon with a parent consoling her daughter."

Sam asked, "Doctor D, I have a stupid question. Let's say JR was up on a ladder and he fell from that height Ryan did. What are the chances he would live?"

"Sam, I've had accidental deaths where someone fell from only 12 feet and died. You can research it and find that some lucky people have fallen from a much higher height than Ryan did and survived with hardly a scratch. It's not so much the height sometimes but how they landed."

"Thanks Doc. But here's a stupid question for everyone: Lets say JR fell and landed with just some busted ribs or a sprained ankle. I've gone through all this rigamarole to just watch him walk away after I wanted him dead. What would someone do to insure he wasn't walking anywhere again?"

An answer wasn't really necessary but the Doc replied, "There are a few scenarios you can play out. First, if Ryan was a younger man he might have even walked away from the fall. He's 52 and chances are he was going to break something falling from 24 feet. His bones at that age are not what a younger mans are. Trust me I know from experience. The murderer, if there is a murderer, would have been hoping he died on inpact, which may be just what had happened. And if he didn't die the killer could just walk away and try again later."

"The second scenario leaves Ryan laying there with some broken bones but still coherent. Now Sam what would you do if JR fell and was laying there and you wanted him dead?"

Sam replied, "I'd bash him in the head. But wouldn't that show on the autopsy?"

Doctor D smiled. "It did, but how do I know if it happened during his fall or after by someone with intent to kill? And no Sam, you can't just bash someone in the head.. You would have to go to the victim, lift his head up and know pretty much precisely where to impact his head with the concrete to make it realistic. If someone wanted him dead then they knew exactly what to do.

You see Sam, we don't have a witness so all I can do is state the obvious and go by the facts. What you have to realize also is that Ryan may have not been hurt that bad. As I said I know of cases where people have fallen from higher heights and walked away. So I'm going to give you a third scenario: The killer watches Ryan fall. He's not that hurt. Maybe just a sprained ankle? Then what does the killer do?"

Sam and JR had discussed this beforehand and knew the answer. It was Maggie who answered. "The killer would have walked away and tried again later and left this one just as an accident. No one would have been the wiser."

JR agreed with her but stated a fact that hadn't occurred to everyone save for a couple of the detectives. "As Dr.D said before the man was 52 and rode hard, his bones were becoming more brittle with age. Chances are that he would have at least sprained an ankle which as we knew he had much more serious internal damage than that. But if this was a murder the murderer was watching to see how badly he was hurt. Hell, he could have died on impact as the Doctor said. But lets say the murderer had planned this all out and Ryan was hurt but not dead? Ryan was a fairly big, tall muscular man. This guy is tough. Say he had a little life left in him. Who the hell is going to just let someone walk up and crush his skull?"

Maggie was wondering the same thing when she said, " Ryan knew the person."

JR and the gang of S and W detectives were happy Maggie had answered. That included Dr Shapiro though Maggie had no idea why.

JR showed no emotion when he said to Maggie. "Maybe. But the murderer would need to have the patientce of a saint. I do know that we are overlooking one big problem. Now Sam and I said that the ladder could fall but the big question is how do you make a 30 foot ladder fall that's sitting firmly on concrete? Let's say the murderer went and placed it close to edge of the concrete walkway so it was very close to the edge next to the soft dirt is which the report says. Now Ryan who's been a roofer all his life would realize his ladder has been moved as he started down. He never would have placed it close to the edge even with a killer hangover. What we have to do is figure out, if this is a murder now and not an accident, how did the killer move that ladder as Ryan was coming down it and if Ryan was able to walk away or crawl, how did the murderer not leave any clues. I do believe Sam and I will head back to the Wayman's place tomorrow. I have an idea but it's just a far-fetched idea that we'll discuss later. Let's move on.."

JR then asked Michelle to give them what Tina and she had found out in regards to Julia's family.

Maggie found it strange that Michelle needed no notes when she started talking.

"Julia has two sisters, Kristen and Sandra. Kristen is an accounts manager for a WalMart store in Jacksonville here in Florida. She's the oldest at 33 and never married. Pays her bills on time, no vehicle violations and likes to go out on weekends. Going by her credit cards its usually to a Steak House and a bar called GIGI's which is a lesbian bar. Again from her spending records we see no heavy drinking other than a few bottles of wine now and then. She has a gym membership and appears to eat healthy. Phone records indicate she talks to her mom maybe once a week and her sister the same. Usually on Sunday nights. When she was 18 she did join the Army for 4 years which is where she got her degree in accounting. Her grades in school were all A's and B's. I'm betting she joined the military to get her degree paid for."

Maggie just sat there amazed. How did Michelle remember everything and how did they get all this information in less than 24 hours.

"The other sister, Sandra, she's the middle sister, who is 31 years old and works part time for a National chain of Pet Stores as a clerk. Tina has very little information on her. Going by her school grades she was lucky to graduate high school. After graduation she worked for Hospice for a year after a quick CNA course, then was suddenly let go. We have no idea of the reason why, but Tina's working on that. She has never moved out from the mobile home her mother purchased in New Port Richey two years after the fathers accidental death. She has no credit cards or debit cards, just a cell phone. So we're really at a loss when trying to get a read on her. She does have a driver license and has a new Toyota Camry registered in her name. It was bought with some of the money that Julia gave the mom when Ryan's accidental death was approved and the check was cashed.

Now the mom. Her name is Isabella. She started having kids at 25 when she married Johnathon Carpenter. She's 58 now and lives in St.petersburg. From what we see Isabella was a stay at home mom until her husband met his untimely death. Both her and her deceased husband were original Floridians and grew up in North Port, just south of here. Before meeting her husband she was a bartender and took up that profession again after her husband's passing. Now Isabella does have Credit Cards which are maxed out, a debit card with $600.00 in it and drives a newer Toyota Camry also which appears to have been bought at the same times as Sandra's with proceeds from Ryan's Insurance payout. Now her husband did leave her the home, which she sold two years afterwards and an insurance policy worth $50,000. Now most mothers would have taken that $50,000 and put it in the bank and kept it for bills or college for the kids. But at the age of 40, when her husband died, she became a slot machine junkie and not a very good one. The $50,000 was gone in two years so she sells the house it appears for cash and buys the mobile home she and Sandra are living in now. She blew the extra cash she received for the house at the Hard Rock Casino here in Tampa and in Biloxi in no time. So now we have Julia at the age of 15, Sandra at 17, having to move from their 3 bedroom nice rancher into a mobile home park. Kristen by this time had gotten the hell out and was stationed in Germany at this time. It

appears from phone records that Julia and Mom spoke at least once, maybe twice a day. The same for Sandra when Mom's not home. Now the deceased father and husband,who by all accounts was very intelligent and hardworking by what we are seeing. He was three years older making him 43 when he was found drowned in Pass a Grille Beach 18 years ago. Another accident which I'll tell you about in a minute. So from what we see he was a master machinist for a local manufacturing company. He was a smoker, he was a weekend drinker and he made $55,000 a year which was very good money at that time. He and Isabella paid their bills on time and had close to $6,000 in the bank when he died. The house they had bought when Kristen was born would have been paid off in 7 years, so they were doing very well as a family. Now we have no idea how he was as a father since we haven't had time to talk to anyone but from what we see he was a normal Dad who smoked who did like to have beer and a shot on the weekends going by their debit cards. It seems as if it was the perfect Brady Bunch family until he passed away. That in itself was a little strange.

It made all the newspapers around here. From what Tina has found out is that Dad and the family are down at Pass-a-Grill Beach early one morning 18 years ago. It stated they were staying at a friend's time-share for the weekend. It appears everyone was in and out of the water that Saturday morning going back to the room when they wanted something to eat or drink since the time share was located very close to the beach. They hadn't seen Dad for awhile and assumed he was back in the room relaxing. All that changed when a couple from Orlando found Dad in the water face up.

Now Julie. I wish I could tell you something that would throw up some red flags but there is nothing. She did great in school, seems to be outgoing with the pep squad, chess club, and a couple of other after school activities. If her mom had saved the money instead of gambling it away she most likely would have gone to college. After graduation she worked for a hospital in their finance department. We're assuming that a few years later she met Ryan Thompson who was a lot older then she was. They married and seemed to have a great life. The reports show no calls

for domestic abuse or violations of any sort. They took vacations and in the three years she was married to Ryan neither one showed as much as a speeding ticket. It's actually kind of boring. It reminds me of this couple I knew in the Keys. They were the nicest couple. They too had kids and …….."

"Michelle stay focused." Rita told her. Everyone smiled knowing that Michelle had a tendency to wonder.

"Right. So anyway if you're looking for some type of smoking gun, I don't think you'll find it in the paperwork."

JR remained silent for a minute when she finished. "Well that was not what I was hoping for. But you ladies did a great job. Now tell us about the interview. Maggie had expected Michelle to continue but instead Michelle asked Tim to play the recording. Starting at when they entered, the taped conversation was basically useless. Julie was polite and answered all their questions politely and didn't seem surprised or upset when Maggie came in nor did she ask why they were asking about Ryan's death. No, she had no idea where Ryan's ladder was, No, she had no idea where the tiles were and No she had no idea if he had any enemies. It was Julie's Mother who started questioning their intentions.

"Is your assumption that both Julie's husbands were killed and weren't accidental deaths? We thought you were here for Jim's death."

"Not at all, we're just covering all of the bases. We will get to Jim's. It's policy when two husbands die accidental deaths to question everything one more time. And again, Julie, let us apologize. We know this is rough on you so let's leave you alone and schedule a time to come back. We'll call you before we come over to make sure it's convenient."

It was at that time Michelle asked if she could use their bathroom saying that there was no way she was going to make it to a gas station. Michelle was explained where the nearest bathroom was by the mother who at this point seemed agitated that they had come to the house and upset Julie. The mother also went to watch Michelle walk down the hallway to insure she found the right door. What was strange is that the

mother stayed in the end of the hallway waiting for Michelle as if she didn't trust her.

Saying their goodbyes ,Maggie apologized again for their intrusion.

Looking at JR , Michelle said, "Sorry honey. I didn't expect it to go like it did either but I'm telling everyone that Julie was a perfect example of a grieving wife. Maggie, do you agree?"

Maggie hadn't expected to be asked her opinion so she took her time answering. "I've been lied to by so many people in the insurance field that it's almost second nature to just expect it. But having recently found someone I care about I believe I would behave exactly as Julie did."

Sam, never one to pass up an opportunity, reminded Maggie that he was married and that though most women felt like she did, it would only be a waste of her time to keep having feelings for him. He only had eyes for Rita.

It took Maggie only a few seconds of disbelief before answering. He had got her and left her speechless. Everyone was waiting for her comeback.

"Sam, I know you're older than some of the rocks around here and your mind is going and soon you will need to have your diapers changed. But for now let me say I was talking about a real man that's next to me. And what I haven't told you is that your wife knew I was in the insurance field and asked me if I would go with her to pick out a very cheap nursing home where the death rate is high. So keep talking shit."

For once Sam was speechless. "Touche." For the next few seconds laughter filled the air along with comments congratulating Maggie for burning Sam. What Maggie failed to notice was Sam looking at JR and Rita giving a smile and slight nod as if to say, she'll do. JR waited till the laughter had died down before asking Rita what she thought of Julie.

"JR, these two are absolutely correct. Julie, I have a feeling isn't involved. These might be actual accidents." Looking at a tall rather geekish lookin tall man Rita asked, "Tim, how did they respond when they left? WAIT, shit almost forgot. Maggie, we need you to sign a confidentiality form before we continue."

Phil, who Maggie knew was the office manager, produced a form he had in a backpack. To Maggie it was pretty simple. Anything S and W said or did was confidential. If she revealed anything she would face a lawsuit or worse. It was simple and to the point. Looking at her Jimmy she asked him about signing. "Honey I signed two years ago and have been working with S and W since then part time but can't discuss it with you because of the form. So sign it and we can talk about everyone here, including Sam."

That was all it took. Maggie signed gladly.

Rita continued. "Okay Tim, tell me you heard something. Anything, Throw a dog a bone, please."

"Shit. I wish I could throw you anything but as of now we got nothing. After the ladies left Mom fixed Julie a nice cup of tea to relax her after you ladies left and there was a call from Kristen to Mom. Nothing exciting there except Mom did tell her that this bitch from

Ryan's first insurance claim was back asking questions. Other than that it's as quiet as a morgue over there."

JR along with Sam was smiling. "You say Mom called Maggie here a bitch?"

"Yep. And didn't say it pleasantly either." Everyone knew by now why JR was smiling.``Perfect" was all he said. Rita said everyone had enough fun for one day so lets eat, then call it a day and meet first thing tomorrow morning to plan out the day. Maggie was sitting there still trying to figure out what JR had meant by "Perfect" . Perfect how? She was actually starting to become a little pissed off that here she was, supposed to be in charge, and knew less than anyone here.

"Excuse me JR. I have a few questions if you don't mind." JR gave his boyish smile and said,

"Of course. Ask away."

"First off, would you please tell me what the hell is going on and why were not even researching the accident of the last one? How the hell do you plan on finding out if this was murder or not?"

"Maggie I'm sorry. We're so used to working this way without a third party such as yourself being in charge we forget. Let me bring you up to

date first by explaining our intentions then will see if you agree. Now Julie's last husband blew himself up in the garage that was located behind Julie's house. Dr. Shapiro will share all the information we have on his laptop when I'm sure you'll be sharing a room? Now every department in the State has been investigating it and found that the welding tanks he was using in a confined area had a leak and built up gas and when he lit a cigarette, Poof. No more husband. Now if we go with the facts which are the same for both accidents we have nothing. Zilch, Nada, Nothing. Now if these aren't accidents then how are we going to prove it? Remember, we also have nothing to go on."

JR was looking at Maggie who was more confused now than ever. Becoming somewhat serious he continued.

"Now your company and one other are paying us only if we can prove these aren't accidents which going by what we have now, they are. We could go through every scenario and look for a hidden clue which we may never find which in turn makes us lose a hell of a lot of money in wasted time. Now I believe that who ever committed these murders, and as I keep saying they may be accidents, we have nothing, so what were going to do is go over what everyone has and see what they missed. As for a plan, let's sleep on it and who knows, maybe something will come to us. Maggie looked at JR as if he was a few cards short of a full deck. "Maggie, later tonight read everything we have on this case and you'll see I'm right. But I need you to trust us. By tomorrow this time we may be able to tell you if were wasting our time or we have a murder to solve."

For the first time in a long time she was happy. All of her hard work would be paying off very soon and she could live her life the way she was supposed to. Knowing that the insurance companies had hired an outside investigating company called S and W, which had been researched, and found out they were Five Star. That's what she wanted.

The light at the end of the tunnel was getting closer.

Chapter 6

The next morning came too early for Maggie. She had stayed up late reading everything on her Doc's laptop computer and there was a lot. She was still amazed that S and W could accumulate this much info in 24 hours. After reading she had to agree with JR. The facts pointed to both being 100 pure accidents. Arriving downstairs she found it was just her Doc, Sam, Rita, JR, Michelle holding Lil Sammy who of course had the dog Venus sitting besides him and Tina the IT young lady. Of course the two dogs gave her the once over. Sam and JR were talking into a speaker phone located on the patio table giving some last minute details Maggie was assuming. She heard everyone's voice who she had met last night signing off. Sam, seeing Maggie, asked if Doctor D kept her up too late. Maggie was still waking up and just flipped him the bird and said she needed coffee. She watched as JR bent down and gave Lil Sammy a kiss followed by an explanation to GD dog that he couldn't come and he'd be home soon and next time he could go. Kissing their wives good-bye she wondered where they were going. She decided on coffee first then an explanation. And it better be a pretty damn good explanation . For Christ's sake, she was supposed to be in charge here.

JR and Sam were headed north to Seminole. Seminole was a town not on the beach, but very close. Located only 20 miles from JR's and Michelle house it still took the two PI's 35 minutes to get there. In this part of Florida when someone described distance to and from a destination it was usually done in time, not miles. Someone could live 8 miles from you and still average 15 to 25 minutes from you. The traffic, lights, speed limits were all a factor. And the season. Come winter when all the tourists and snow birds were in Florida enjoying the warm weather, an 8 mile drive could take you 30 minutes or longer. Traffic became a free for all once all those warm weather seekers from up north came down.

Arriving at the address they were given the two men looked at each other and their expressions said it all. Expecting just a small Florida home on an oversized lot they were very disappointed. Michelle had said an Aunt had left Jim the house. Calling Michelle and asking he was told again Jim Bane was left the property by an Aunt who had been very successful in real estate and had died in a car accident years ago. Jim, being the only nephew, with no other relatives other than her sister, Jim's mom, she had left Jim at the age of 47 everything when she passed on. Jim had been the sole beneficiary in her will. So at 47, Jim became the owner of a very up-scale 4 bedroom brick rancher. What made it worth the call to Michelle was the property. Jim had close to three acres of the best prime property around. "Michelle? Do you have any idea what this property's worth? Being Michelle and not having a care about property values or never having read about it was clueless.

"No idea. Is it a lot? "

"Honey, this property's gotta be worth close to a million or two to a developer I'm betting. So now if she sells the house and property she is worth over three million dollars in dead husband's accidents funds."

"No kidding. Who would have thought."

Saying their goodbyes, JR just shook his head. Sam just smiled. "You got to love that woman."

Pulling into the drive leading to the house Sam asked JR how he wanted to handle it. After the explanation all Sam said was "Really? I put on my good shoes to dig around in soot? You couldn't tell me to wear pants?" JR just shook his head. He knew Sam only owned one pair of pants and they were black dress pants that Sam used for funerals and weddings.

Sam HAD put on his 'good' boat shoes for meeting Julia and the mother, who they were betting was still there and were right in that assumption. Going to the front door Sam and JR put on their best serious face to show their sorrow. Knocking only once the front door was immediately opened by an older woman they assumed was the Mom as had been described by Michelle.

"Ma'am, we're so sorry to bother you, but we were hired by Harvest Salt Insurance company to take some samples of the soot. Maggie Depew said it would be all right."

Mom stood in the doorway and remained quiet for so long that Sam, being Sam continued, "We won't be but a few minutes and will be in and out in no time if that's okay?"

Sam and JR were starting to wonder if she would ever respond when she said nicely, "Gentleman, you go ahead and do what you have to do. Julie's sleeping but as her mother I give you permission."

Thanking the lady, they left the van out front in the shade and the two followed the drive from the front to the back to see the remains of a burnt out large garage. Some of the burnt supports were still partially there and one of the block walls was partially still standing. Other than that, black and very dark brown soot and lots of it were everywhere with burnt tools and plastic and metal containers thrown throughout.

"JR, did you notice anything about Mom? Other than not asking for our ID's? You think that's a little strange?"

" Maybe but we did mention Maggie's name. I mean look at us. Couple of handsome guys dressed in shorts and Hawaiian shirts. And you looking like a throwback to Woodstock. Now Mom might not be all that bright but anyone would want some kind of identification I would think." JR already knew why Mom didn't care who went back there.

"What do you mean a throwback to Woodstock? I resent that JR."

Looking at the remains Sam asked JR, "Well Einstein, what's next?"

"Sam, remember a couple of months ago when you had that poker game and you won, what? A hundred and some change form everyone in that last hand if I remember correctly. I was watching you Sam, I pretty much knew you didn't have it but still I dropped out."

"Oh yeah! I loved it!" Sam loved playing poker, especially when he won.

"So now what we're going to do is bluff just like you did. ."

"You'll never know that. So how are you going to bluff and pray tell me why we're going to?"

"Sam, Mom didn't ask for our ID's because she could give two shits who came back here. So A, she's not involved or B, she is and knows there is nothing at all to incriminate her. Now we could spend days going through this crap and you know what ? We wouldn't find squat I'm betting. Whoever is planning these accidents has thought of everything. Again we are not even sure their not accidents."

Sam paused thinking about what JR had said. "JR, what does your gut tell you? You usually have that sixth sence, so tell me, is it or aint it murder if you had to say right now? This is just between us."

JR and Sam had worked together for so many cases and 99 percent of the time he was right, but this case had him baffled.

"If I had to make a guess I'd say Julia is not a murderer. It's too close to home. I do have a gut feeling Mom's got a hand in this. But again with this case, shit it could be the milkman who's doing it. 'If it is murder" he said for the umpteenth time.

Sam took it all in and said, "So what's next?"

JR reached into his short pockets and pulled out 6 sandwich bags. "Here Sam, take three and walk around and get some samples. In just a few minutes we'll act like we found something in the pile and make a big to-do about it." Reaching in his other short pockets JR removed 2 sets of gloves

"What? I thought we were just going to look!"

"Where the hell did you think we were going? A tea party?" JR was trying to keep a straight face in case anyone was watching.

"This SUCKS!" Mumbling a few choice words Sam took his three bags and a set of gloves and pretended he was looking and every now and then would take a sample. Five minutes later JR yelled to Sam, "Hey asshole, looks like I found something! Go get the camera out of the Van so I can take pictures before I move it."

"JR, I ain't walking back to the van! It's hot and I smell like soot and I'm ready to go."

"Sam, I called it first so you gotta walk. If you had come up with this idea and called it first then I would have to walk."

Sam looked at JR and just said, "God's going to get you for this." Walking away to get the camera JR could hear Sam mumbling to himself. "Making an old man walk in this heat, shit."

Five minutes after Sam had gone to get the camera, JR realized his mistake. The work vans S and W used were no ordinary work vans. Looking at them from the outside they could fit in with any working van on the road. Inside is where the IT partner Tim had shown his love of gadgets and computer hardware. Taking a small computer stand he had made each van equipped with a computer with a 23" monitor and accessorized with a very comfortable office chair., a small refrigerator and saving the best for last, a very small bathroom with its own holding tank. It was tight but any two partners would be able to work somewhat comfortably for long periods of time. Gadgets from listening devices to camera surveillance were installed. Every available space was utilized. Tim had researched air conditioning systems that were self contained and 12 volt and came up with a unit that could fit and give the maximum BTU output for the Florida weather.

JR took out his cell phone and called Sam. "Where are you Sam? Problems finding the camera?"

"Not at all. By the time I got to the van I was dying for a cup of coffee. So I made one. Why is it getting hot out there?"

"Okay Sam, you got me so get your butt back here!

"Say it."

"No"

"Say it or I'll make another cup." JR knew he would.

"Okay, you're the MAN and I'm a shmo. Happy?"

"No, say it one more time. JR did and 5 minutes later Sam came back looking all refreshed with the camera in one hand and a bottle of water in the other.

"Here you go shmo. Thought you may be getting thirsty." The two spent the next few minutes taking pictures of the item JR had pretended to find. Finished, JR looked at Sam and asked if he had seen any movement in the windows.

"Oh yeah, somebody's watching us." With that said JR turned his back towards the house and bent down picking up a piece of charred wood and quickly put it in the last plastic food bag he had and deposited it in his pocket.

Sam casually glanced around and turned back to JR, " Somebody saw you." The Bluff Game was beginning. On the way back to the house Sam asked JR what his actual plan was. JR took his time answering.

"Sam, I'm actually starting to think that these may be murders. There is just way too much money involved. And two husbands accidentally killed in three years? Maybe Julie is capable, who knows. But if she isn't then that leaves the sisters, another relative, someone who wants Julia to be miserable or the milkman."

"Can't be the milkman, they did away with those years ago as far as I know."

"Okay, we can cross the milkman off. But if these aren't accidents then it's someone close to Julia. Now for what reason I don't know yet. But what are the top reasons for people to kill someone?'

"Money, revenge and love. Everyone knows that."

"Right Sam, but I don't think this is a jealous lover. And Tina found nothing about revenge. There's too much moolah involved. So my bets are on the money."

"Then you're back to Julia. She's the only one making any money. I mean she gives some to the family but the big money is in Julia's account." JR who was driving just turned to Sam and gave him a smirk.

"Really Sam? There's no other way?"

Sam had to think about it. Looking at JR he finally said, "You think?"

"Maybe, now while I'm driving I need you to make some phone calls to get this rolling." At the same time Sam was asking JR about his plan, Michelle and the ladies were sitting on the lanai discussing their plans for the day. Until JR figured out what was the plan everyone was at a stand still. With the ladies showered and ready to head out for some baby clothes shopping, or at least that was the excuse, when Maggie asked

Michelle exactly what was the plan. Maggie was still in the dark and didn't realize JR needed time to figure it out.

"Well we're not going to catch them. What JR is doing is just going through the motion right now. JR knows he and Sam are wasting their time. If something was going to be found the police or Fire Marshall would have found it."

"Ahh, Michelle? What exactly is the plan then? Because it sounds like S and W have nothing so far." Maggie was beginning to worry that maybe they were all wasting their time. Michelle, Rita and Tina just chuckled. "Maggie, relax. This evening we'll know if they are murders or accidents. Then I'm betting if it was murder, you will have your murderer within 48 hours. Then you'll be able to go tell Michael Wood that you solved the case and try and recover your $450,000 . And Raymond Gant will be $750,000 dollars richer, minus our fee and you'll get a raise. Sweet."

Maggie was still confused. "Michelle, you just agreed that S and W have nothing, so please tell me how you folks plan on doing that? Shouldn't we be doing something?"

"Oh no, we'd just be wasting our time and us folks won't figure it out. Oh NOOO. No, that"s where JR comes in. I was surprised he didn't really have a clue what he was going to do this morning. It usually comes to him in the early morning. I guess he had other things on his mind this morning." Michelle gave the ladies a wink.

Rita said "Michelle" in a motherly tone, like scolding a teenager. As the ladies finished the last of their coffee and were just heading off to grab their purses and Lil Sam's baby things, Sam called Rita. Rita told him who was there and put Sam on speaker.

"Hey ladies. It's Sam and I have a great story to tell. It is so funny how I outsmarted JR. You guys will love it."

The ladies could hear JR in the background saying, "Later Sam.."

"Shit JR, you just don't want me to tell the story. So I'll make you happy. Ladies, JR, who I've taught all my skills and gave him my guidance has come up with a plan finally. I had it figured out earlier but it finally came to him." The ladies had grins on their faces knowing Sam didn't have a clue.

"So first Thomas and Katie are on their way over, Phil said he could spare them and second, Tina what's your low life boyfriend doing today? Is he coming home?" Tina told Sam that he was still diving with some friends. Everyone knew but Maggie that he wasn't diving but up in Delaware on company business..

"He deserves it. He did a hell of a job on the last case. Both of you did. Hey hold on." Sam was listening to something JR said. "Hey Maggie, what's Dr. Death doing today? He plans on coming over to smooch with you?" Maggie blushed, AGAIN, while the ladies turned to her smiling.

"As a matter of fact Sam he is. He took the next couple of days off so we can 'smooch' while I'm here."

"Great, call him and tell him we need his help and you'll give him a big smooch if he does. Tell him we need him there asap. And Maggie, if you guys have kids remember Lil Sams taken. You could call him Lil Dr Death." Sam thought it was funnier than hell.

"Hey Tina, JR wants to ask if you would go into the computer room and boot up and then call back. He needs a few things if you're not busy." Tina would never be too busy. The computers were her world.

She thought back to how much work and time she had put into finally achieving her goal. She learned everything she could about murders, robberies and other bullshit crimes commited daily in the world and the mistakes criminals had made. Most of it involved reading the internet and watching the news or the countless documentaries on every channel looking for ratings. So many stupid people who rushed out to kill someone with no or very little thought on how to accomplish the perfect murders. Idiots who deserved to be caught. What was perfect was that they, the news reporters, the folks who did the documentaries and God love the internet, always said how they were caught. How smart the detectives were who finally solved the crime.

Everything was right there in front of them telling them what not to do, but again Idiots with no patience to research, to plan just the thought

of killing someone. How many countless times has someone been caught by a neighbor's camera as someone uses a vehicle to move a body? And if you kill someone for Christ sake, put them in 3 layers of good sturdy Garden bags. You can buy a box of 25 for $7.99 at the dollar store. Spend a little time and just a few dollars to do it right. And don't put them in a dumpster.

Better yet, make it look like an accident.

Chapter 7

"Okay ladies we'll be there in a little bit and JR's going to tell you his great plan. Adios amigos."

By the time JR and Sam pulled in the drive, two other additional vehicles were already there. Sam looked at JR smiling, "Damn Dr. D really wants to smooch."

Arriving the guys had been expecting to find everyone out by the lanai but instead found them in the dining room.

"Hey, what's everyone doing in here? It's beautiful out there!"

"Sam it's 90 degrees out there already! Sit your ass down there and JR you stand there and tell us your plan." When Rita took charge, Rita took charge, no arguing.

Thomas a black gentleman who looked to be in his mid 50'said "Yeah Sam, sit your old ass down."

Rita looked at both Thomas and then Sam and said, "You two, no messing around. We have guests so set a good example."

"Dr. D's a guest? Shit, I bought that new fishing rod and reel from the money I took off him in poker games."

Dr. Shapiro looked at Maggie and said, "He cheats." Sam laughed and was starting to say something when Rita looked at both Sam, Thomas and Dr. Shapiro and said, "Hush, all of you now. JR tell us what's up before these morons go at it."

For some reason Maggie was starting to feel comfortable around everyone and had a feeling she was about to see real detectives, no matter how maladjusted they were, at work.

"Thanks Rita. And thank you Dr. Shapiro and Katie, Thomas for all of you coming to help us out. Listen to make it short and sweet, we are not going to find squat going the way we're going right now. We could look for clues but come on. This aint CSI, and Sams not Magnum and Rita and Michelle aren't Cagney and Lacey. There may be evidence but as Sam would say, 'It's like finding a needle in a haystack. So today I'm standing out there in the heat and I started thinking: Everyone says that there is no perfect murder. And thought how do we know that? If its a perfect murder then no one would ever know cause Its perfect. A perfect murder would not be a murder, but a murder that appeared as an accident. Maggie, how many accidental deaths does your company handle a year? Lots I bet. And you know if I had to murder someone and had the time and was fairly intelligent I'd make it look like an accident. Not murder. With murder, everyone's looking. An accidental death? Well planned with lots of patience, That's the way to go.``

Michelle spoke up and said for JR to please get to the point. They all knew it was an accidental death that may be murder. How the hell were they going to find out if it was.

JR gave Michelle a "yes dear" and continued. "Katie, you've heard everything from yesterday, let's hear who we're looking for if it's not an accidental death."

Maggie had watched as Thomas and Katie had come in. She had no idea what Katie's specialty was but would soon find out that Katie was a profiler for the FBI and worked for both S and W and the government in an agreement made with S and W made a couple of years back. Now she mainly worked for S and W but kept her credentials with the FBI. As a tall latino lady she had the air of a doctor which Maggie would find out shortly she was when she questioned Rita afterwards. Her Doc had told her last night that the gentleman called Thomas was a retired police officer from up north and a hell of a detective.

Katie didn't hesitate. " All right, let's assume it's not accidental. Now what this person is more than anything is detail oriented if you haven't figured that out. And intelligent. Very intelligent when it comes to making murder appear as an accident. Hearing how the first husband died my first thought was maybe a big strong guy was hired to push the ladder over while Ryan was on it but if it was murder they would have to know Ryan's schedule, his working habits and I cant see this murderer having a strong guy on call. Plus what's the chance of the person they hired talking? No, this is all done by a person that knew both dead husbands personally. And like JR said, looking at both accidents its going to be hard to prove they were both murder when we have no clues."

JR waited till Katie had finished and asked one last question. "Katie, if you had to decide if this was done for money or lust or anything else under the sun, what would you say?"

Again Katie didn't hesitate. "Oh this is all about the money in my opinion.Now I'm saying you need to really look at Julia closer. She's the one benefiting from this. What got me confused is that most women who are psychopaths, and I believe that's what you're dealing with, kill with poison to make it look accidental.

JR smiled. "Thanks Katie. I would really appreciate it if instead of Michelle and Rita you went and interviewed Julia and her Mom this afternoon with Maggie. Michelle, I'd like you and Rita to interview Sandra at the same time. Thomas our plane is in for preventive maintenance but I'd like you and Sam to take a charter to Jacksonville and interview Kristen. You guys decide what questions to ask her. Now I had Tina pull up all the sister's work schedules and if they hold to them as in the past we should be able to interview the sister and Mom at between 3:30 and 4. The one sister Kristen, you're just going to have to wing it and hope she'll see you. All right then, that should put everyone back here at the latest by 7 tonight. We'll have a late supper and discuss everything then. Now in just a few minutes Dr. Schipero and I will be going over to see Doctor Blake who performed the autopsy on Mom's husband who died accidentally 18 years

ago.." Everyone had a million questions but remained silent wondering where JR was going with all this.

"Oh, and Tim and Laurie will be coming over to talk with Michelle and Rita. Also I'm requesting that everyone as of now start carrying."

Sam was serious for a change when he asked, "JR, what the hell? You think it could come to that?"

"No, but why take chances. And Katie I agree, this is for money. This kind of money makes people do some strange things. One last thing, we thought this was all about the insurance money but that property that Jim Bane's house sits on is worth how much Tina?"

"One point seventy five millions. And it's going up each day'"

JR let that number set in. "So now we're up to over two point five million and I wouldn't be surprised if the deceased didn't have a few investments left to him by his Aunt when she passed away. This Julie is going to be a very wealthy woman. That kind of money makes people do very bad things to keep it."

The afternoon came and went quickly for everyone. By 7 pm everyone was back at home base aka Michelle and JR's house.

Tina who had watched Lil Sam had handed him back to Michelle when she came in the door said, "Michelle I don't know much about kids but the little guy only cried once when he was hungry. I swear it wasn't really a cry but just enough for him to say he was hungry. And Venus never left his side. I've seen some weird shit but this is getting fucking spooky."

Next in were Katie and Maggie who appeared normal but both went to the kitchen and made margaritas talking as if they were old friends. Jr and Dr. Shapiro both coming in next looking for the loves of their life and finding Michelle and Maggie acted as if they had been gone for days. JR of course was followed closely by GD dog and when he bent to kiss lil Sam in Michelle's arm had to give a kiss and pay some attention to him. Talking to GD dog for a minute and scratching behind his ears and the dog was fine. Lastly was Thomas and Sam.

Thomas looked as if he had been dragged through the bushes. Sam looked ready to set the world on fire.

JR wanted to hear what everyone had to say but knew showers and a few minutes of down time would refresh everyone . Once seated JR said he and Dr. D would go first. Followed by Sam and Thomas, then Rita and Katie followed by Michelle and Maggie. Lastly would be Tim and Laurie Looking around he saw Tim, their IT guy smiling and biting at the bit to say something. "Tim, did you and Laurie come up with something interesting?"

"Oh yeah, but you guys go ahead and will follow up." By the gleam in his and Laurie's eyes and the big smile, everyone from S and W knew things were about to get interesting. Maggie was wondering what the hell Tim and his wife Laurie could have come up with while they were gone. They were computer hardware geeks as far as she knew. It must have something to do with the bug in Julie's house; she wasn't supposed to see Rita placed under the end table when Michell asked to use the bathroom.

JR started. "We'll the Doc here and myself went to the coroner's home who performed the autopsy on Johnathon Carpenter, Mom's deceased husband who accidentally drowned you'll remember. His name is Dr. George Blake looks as old as the hills, but his mind is still sharp. To make a long story short, he remembered the drowning well since everyone was a big time interest back then and it made front page news in the Tampa newspaper. He and the Doc here talked about some medical mumbo jumbo which I had a hard time following which basically came down to Mom's husband being drunk as a skunk. And not drunk but DRUNK DRUNK. His alcohol reading was over the chart. Dr. Blake said he couldn't figure out how he even got into the water. Dr. Blake also said the autopsy showed everything normal as far as the heart, which showed wear from smoking but was still in decent shape, and even his brain looked normal. He figured that maybe he had a brain aneurysm that he just couldn't find. Accidental Death, this is what he told the papers and put on the death certificate.

Now I figured that's it, until our man here, Dr. D says to Dr. Blake, 'Okay George, give me the scope.' Dr. Blake looks at our man here and says after

looking at me then back to Dr. D., "Off the record?" That's when I started recording.

JR handed Tim a tape. Putting it in the mini tape player it began. " I knew from the beginning there was something strange about this drowning. I've been here my whole life and became a coroner right out of college. I know about drowning from pools and especially drowning at the beach. Looking at everything and doing it by the book points to this man drowning but to be honest I just had this feeling that something was missing. Now what I included on the autopsy report was that he had on dive boots, the kind made to wear with fins. Now what got me as strange was where were the fins? I mean some folks wear dive boots to protect themselves from sharp rock and shells but that's not the norm. And it was too slight to even include but to me it looked as if pressure had been put on both ankles. It could have been from the fin straps too but all these years and you showing up, it still bothers me. But again where were the fins? I had the police ask his wife and she said that he had brought them but they were still in the car."

"Okay I'm not an expert on drowning, but Dr.. Blake, you're saying it could have been someone holding him under the water by his ankles to drown him?"

"Possible? Yes. Plausible? No. People on the beach would have seen a big guy coming up from the water to the beach and I'm saying big guy because this guy would have to be over 250 lbs and muscular. People no matter how intoxicated will fight to survive and get air. Know that if someone held him under he was a very big person. That's why I just let it go. It was one of those that could have, maybe, or not. I choose not to. And think about if I would have written it. I'd be the laughing stock of Florida. I pictured the headlines, Corner says Big Mermaid came up and drowned Johnathon Carpenter. And really gentlemen, this was all speculation. I had no proof." Everyone listening had a feeling Doc Blake was feeling doubts..

After the tape finished Sam spoke up and asked JR what he thought. "Sam, shit, I wish I could tell you. What do you think?"

"I think I need another beer." As Sam went to retrieve another beer JR was grinning as he asked Thomas how the interview went with Kristen in Jacksonville.

"Listen, I've known Sam for years and he still finds a way to grate on my last nerves. Let me tell you about my day. First we had that two prop plane Tina got for us out of St. Pete's airport which was how do I say it? A piece of shit. Tina, I don't know what kind of deal you got but trust me it was like flying in a 69 Nova that hadn't been taken care of."

"Sorry, it was the best I could get on such short notice and you know our plane was in for inspection. So I did my best. And what's a 69 Nova?"

"I know you did your best and I could live with it but I got Sam bitching the entire flight saying 'This sucks' "Where's the beer and peanuts?" The man didn't stop whining the whole flight. The 45 minutes it took to get there seemed like a 6 hour flight."

"Yeah Tina! Did we piss you off?" Sam had come back in and caught the tail end of the conversation.

"I just told Thomas, it was the best I could do on short notice. Next time you boneheads can drive!"

Thomas continued, "So I had a delightful plane ride with shithead there and we landed and we went to the car rental dealer and lo and behold, Tina's got us a small compact car. Now I'm 5'10" but lurch there is 6' 3"and gets in and he looks like a scrunched up grasshopper sitting on the end of a stick. I almost felt sorry for him. Almost. The big lug there is whining like a 5 year old. 'I can't breathe, the seats are hurting my balls, why did Tina do this to us? I heard everything for the next 55 minutes till we arrived at Walmart" .

"I thought it was only 25 minutes to Kristen's?"' Rita asked.

"It is. Sam was so pissed he put Snow Street in the GPS instead of Snow Avenue. We had to backtrack 30 minutes.."

"Tina, are you sure you didn't do this on purpose?" Sam asked, giving her a questionable look.

Rita gave Sam that let it go look and said none to politely, "Sam, she said she didn't! Now let Thomas finish. We now know you two did finally make it there so what did she say?" Rita was trying to keep a straight face. Sam kept quiet but was eying not just Tina, but all the women questionably.

"So we get there late and I'm thinking she's not here and gone already and shit, now we're stuck driving to her house with this ass hole bitching and complaining the whole time when for some reason here comes Kristen out the main doors of Walmart. She's running late too. I'm thinking maybe things are looking up. So we get out and walk over to her and introduce ourselves by showing her our PI identification and giving her one of Maggie's cards. Now remember were in the front of the Walmart parking lot and I've got Sam standing there in Bermuda shorts and that Hawaiian shirt in boat shoes looking stupid and asked her if she would mind taking a few questions about her sister and her deceased husband Jim Bane. At first I thought she was going to say Fuck you guys then she asked, "What's this all about? "

" I go ahead and explain that this is all protocol and we're working for Maggie and her company. So your Miss Kristen is eying us like we must be lepers then for some reason her attitude changed. She said she had a couple of minutes before she had to meet someone at the gym so ask away. So I start by asking her if she knew if Jim had any enemies. She says politely "No, but that she and Julie weren't that close and hardly stayed in touch. Then I asked her if Julie ever mentioned if Jim Bane and herself got along. She says the same thing, Her and Julie hardly talked. I asked her about the first husband then and she said pretty much the same thing. She did say she had been at their wedding and thought that Ryan appeared to be a great guy. It was then she asked us why we were asking about Ryan's death. So here I am standing with Jimmy Sam Buffet asking all the right questions and getting ready to explain that this was just protocol when out of the blue he says, "Hey girl, I got a question: What the hell happened to good ole dad?"

Kristen just standing there willing to talk and Sam asked this fucked up question. Now we have 'Kristen looking like a jolt of electricity just ran through her and after a few seconds tells us politely, "Fuck off you pieces

of shit". Followed by a threat of the police if we ever came near her again. This lady was pissed but she kept her composure, I'll give her that. She just turns around and walks to her car. Now here we are looking like a couple of idiots and I have to travel back with Ace 'Grumpy old Man' Sam here. The only good thing is he was getting tired so he stopped bitching pretty much. Now here we are having wasted a day of my life with nothing to show for it besides a killer headache." Everyone was looking at Sam. JR knew that Sam never did anything without a good reason..

"What? You think I went too far?" Sam was enjoying himself. "All right let me explain to you rookies what we found out. Thomas, answer me this my friend: Say we stood there for another 15 minutes and you asked her another dozen questions. What do you think Kristen's response would be to anything you asked her? I'll tell you. 'I don't have any communication with my sister other than talking to her once every month or so just to say hello.' We could talk to her in a dark room with a 150 watt bulb shining in her eyes and that's what she would say. Kristen wasn't giving us anything. Now by asking her about her father out of the blue we know a lot. Katie, you're the smart one in this group when it comes to reading people. You want to explain to them what we learned when I asked her that question?"

Katie was the psychologist that had dealt with her share of unstable murderers, rapist and most other felonies with her time in the FBI and could read people where most people couldn't.

"All right Sam but let me ask my better half here first a few questions. Thomas you said that when you met Kristen she appeared reluctant then she changed."

"Yes. That's what I said. It appeared to me like when we first introduced ourselves she was ready to just walk away then her attitude changed. You could see it in her face." Thomas wasn't sure what she was getting at.

"When you asked her those first questions you said she replied politely. Would you say she took her time answering like she was thinking about them or did they just come out quickly?" Thomas took his time thinking back before answering. "The first couple of questions she had answered

like she was thinking and then she did appear to answer faster. I assumed it was because she was becoming familiar with us."

"And you said she asked you about why you were asking questions about the first husband's death after she answered a couple of questions about him first?" Again Thomas answered "Yes".

"Honey, more than anything I would love for Sam to be wrong but I believe he did the right thing by asking about her father when he did. Maybe he went about it the wrong way but I have to agree with Sam on this one. This lady knew you were going to be asking those questions, it appears."

"What? No way. This lady was willing to talk."

"Honey, you may be right but you're looking at it that way because one, she's good and you were trying to read her and thinking what your next question would be. Sam had the luxury of just standing there listening and watching. If roles were reversed then you would have seen what Sam heard and saw and probably would have done the same thing. I really do hate to admit it but I believe Sam's right."

Sam who could have said something to grate on Thomas's nerves became serious, or what amounted to Sam being serious. "Katie's right Thomas. And you're also right about me being an asshole today. It seems that it was just one of those days where everything that could go wrong went wrong. I do believe there were other factors involved in this adventure starting with the shitty plane to that small compact car and if there were I'm going to find out." Sam said that last part as he eyed Tina.

"Sam, let it go. Tina told you it was quick notice so forget about it."

"Quick notice my ass."

"Sam let it go and got to the bottom line with Kristen. What was your take on her? And give us the quick version. We have more to go over."

After stating one last time he was going to find out if there was any mischief afoot Sam did finally continue. "Our Kristen knows more than she's saying in my opinion. It may be something hidden in the family closet or as Thomas said he may be I'm reading too much into this but there is something there. When she didn't ask why Thomas was asking about the

first husband's death until after he had asked a couple questions about it I could tell she might know something. As I said before all she had to keep saying is she didn't know anything and she couldn't go wrong. BUT put yourself in her shoes or anyone's shoes for that matter. A couple of guys show up and are asking questions about your brother-in laws accidental death. Out of the blue the guy asking the questions starts asking about the previous brother in law's accidental death. Now I believe, and I could be wrong, the first question I would ask is why the hell are you asking about his death? Kristen didn't. Her second mistake I feel was when I asked her about her fathers death. Thomas, you remember what she said? She says Fuck Off and if we ever came near her again she would call the police. Now again, put yourself in anyone's shoes being asked about your fathers accidental drowning years before. Are you going to just say Fuck Off and I'll call the police if you come near me again? It's possible but again I'd ask what the hell my fathers death had to do with the accidental death of my brother in law. I'd like to know. Bottom line is I believe Kristen knows some things she won't talk about."

Everyone was taking in what Sam had told them when JR said that the two had done an excellent job and asking Rita and Michelle what they had come up with.

"We had a great day. We did lunch and got a little shopping in for the decorations for the 4th. Rita bought Lil Sam the cutest outfit. It's red, white and blue with..."

"Michelle,sweetie, you are wondering again." Rita told her.

"Right. Sorry. I'll show everyone later. At about 3:45 we show up at Sandra's place of work and I'm wishing I had brought GD Dog and Venus because it's one of those pet stores where you can have dogs go in to shop with you. We go inside and ask for the manager and tell her we would like to see Sandra Carpenter. The manager who was as nice as could be looked at us and said she would page her. Now Rita and I, unlike some folks here, were dressed professionally and we even carried briefcases so we looked important. A couple of minutes later and Sandra appears eying us suspiciously. We introduced ourselves and showed her our PI badges and

gave her one of Maggies cards. By this time everyone's looking at us trying to figure out what the heck she's doing with us. Rita asked if we could step outside or somewhere we could talk privately and I believe Sandra agreed just so everyone would stop staring. Once outside we walked down to a spot where we felt Sandra would feel more comfortable being out of prying eyes. Rita began by apologizing saying again how this was just protocol and thanking her for taking the time to see us. I have to say she didn't appear that upset or even surprised to see us. She was calm and answered all of Rita's questions. Now as with Sandra we received pretty much the same answers as what Kristen said. She was not that close to Julie but as far as she knew her and Jim had the perfect relationship. Even when Rita questioned her about Ryan's death she remained perfectly calm asking if we thought this could be something besides an accident with the husbands deaths. She did ask this as Rita brought up Ryan's death and Rita of course explained to her that it was just standard routine questions seeing how two husbands died accidental deaths in less than three years.

She was a model sister when it came to answering our questions. The only time she faltered was when at the end and Rita was again apologizing for our intrusion she mentioned that this must really be hard for Julie especially with her father dying years ago in an accident too. It looked as if for some reason she was caught off guard. Like we weren't supposed to know about that. It could have been my imagination but talking about it afterwards Rita said she felt it too. After a moment she says, "Yeah, she's had some bad luck. I'm not sure how she can deal with everything. It's got to be hard. She just seems so depressed now." And that was it. I have it taped if anyone wants to hear it. But in our opinion other than the last question about her Dad it went exactly as you would expect an interview to go."

JR thanked the two for doing a great job but said he had one question. " You said when Sandra first met you two she eyed you suspiciously. Do you think she was surprised you two were there?"

"Rita and I talked about that on the way home and we honestly can't say. You have to meet Sandra. She's one of those people that just maintains a

steady monologue. She reminded me of that comedian we saw on cable whose voice stays the same no matter what he's talking about."

"Got it.I like that guy. Okay Maggie, Katie, your turn."

The two looked at each other and Katie nodded at Maggie. "I wish we could tell you we had a productive afternoon but the opposite is true. Katie and I arrived unannounced at about 4:10. Mom answers the door and says she wished we would have called first since Julie had a very rough night sleeping and was so depressed and that Julie was taking a nap and really didn't want to wake her up. I told her we understood and would she mind if we asked her a few questions.. She agreed and I started with probably the same questions everyone here asked the two sisters. Did she know if Julie and Jim had marital problems? Did she know if Jim was a big drinker? Did Jim have enemies? Each question I asked was pretty much followed by some type of excuse for not being able to tell us anything. We heard that she tried not to get too involved in her daughter's lives, then she said it's probably best to ask Julie when she's awake and feeling better. She came up with every excuse to not give us a direct answer. Before we had time to bring up her husband's accidental death she brought it up saying that first Julie had to deal with her fathers accidental drowning death, then Ryans and now Jim's death she could understand why Julie was so depressed. It was such a shame that now she had to deal with the insurance company bringing it all up again. In a nutshell we have nothing."

Everyone looked at JR when he asked for Maggie to repeat what she had just said about Julie being depressed. Maggie was wondering what the hell she had missed. Repeating it JR asked Maggie why Mom said it.

Maggie was confused. "Why did she say that?"

"Yes. I mean did you ask her a question or did she just say it?" Maggie had to think about it and looked at Katie. "I believe it just came up as she was explaining. Katie has the tape if you want to play it."

JR was lost in another world for a few moments while everyone waited. "All right, it doesn't matter. We have bigger issues right now. Tim, please tell me you've heard Julie's voice recently."

"Yeah, we just heard her and Mom discussing something to do with water. Julie seems groggy."

Maggie looking at Tim closely could see a small headphone in his left ear. She had assumed it was for his telephone. Now how the hell could he know what Mom and Katie were saying.

"Tim, you stayed glued to that for now. We will go ahead and set it up in the computer room after we're done here and we will take shifts listening. Now Laurie you go ahead and give us the quickest run down of what Tim and you have heard. Shit, wait."

Phil, you have everyone on line?" Maggie hadn't realized it but JR was talking into a pineapple and Phil the office manager was replying from it. "Almost. Should be on in the next few minutes."

"Thanks now, let's meet back here in say 15 minutes. I know Sam's dying to show Thomas that new fish finder he's got."

Sam and Thomas left with Thomas bitching to Sam about buying a new fish finder since he hadn't even figured out how to work the old one. Maggie was surprised that everyone just carried on as if nothing was going on.

"Rita, what the hell's going on here? Did I miss something? And what's with the pineapple?"

"Oh no. It's just that JR most likely has it figured out. I told you he would. Will know in a few minutes now. The pineapple was Tim's idea. He thought it would be a great conversation piece and fit in with Michelle's décor. Guys a genius."

Dr. D was sitting next to Maggie and saw the confusion written all over her face. "Honey, you look confused. Trust me, I've worked with these guys in the past and they just don't do things like big companies do. There a little more more, how to say this, ah not by the book.

"Jimmy, they don't even know me? What happens since I signed the confidentiality form, I go tell my friends back north about S and W?"

"Maggie, S and W know more about you than I do. You were checked and rechecked before you were invited into their home. They know everything about you. And as far as talking, they know you won't because

one you like them and would never jeopardize their business and two, they would ruin anyone who interferes with S and W. You have no idea what S and W is worth and the money needed to ruin you or I if we talked would be just a drop in a bucket with their resources."

"Okay that I understand. But Jimmy,why me? I'm nobody. They really didn't even need me here."

"Honey everything S and W does has a hidden meaning which in time they will tell you. Now relax and let's have a drink and wait for JR."

JR had taken a walk with Michelle and GD Dog while Rita watched Lil Sam. Holding hands Michelle chatted about her day with Rita and some of the decorations she had bought and what she planned on doing for food for the upcoming party. GD was following closely besides the two. JR found it so relaxing and listened with little thought of their next move. Time had shown JR that relaxing with Michelle or GD dog gave his brain the chance to step back and when he did think about a case it usually came in stronger after a few minutes of tranquility. Before the two knew it 15 minutes had passed and the three went back to find everyone waiting for them.

"Tim, what's happening?"

" They finished dessert and now they're just watching TV. Julie sounds like she's in another world.."

"That's interesting. Laurie, please go ahead and tell us what happened." Laurie was Tim's better half and the two, like every couple who worked for S and W, could almost read each other's mind it seemed. Both in their late 30's they made an ideal couple with Tim being somewhat of a geek and Laurie being more carefree. Between the two they were a perfect match.

"We have tapes of everything but the real excitement came at 4 and 4 :30. I could tell you but let me play the tapes and you can see that you got something going on." Laurie started the small recorder and turned the volume up so everyone could hear it. For a small recorder the sound was excellent. Laurie fast forwarded to the part where everyone could hear a phone ringing, then mom's voice: "Hello?" Silence " Slow down honey and take your time." Silence

"I told you I wouldn't be surprised if they stopped by." Silence "What?" Mom sounded surprised then. Silence "What did they say about your father?" Now Mom sounded pissed! Silence

"Good answer. Now what else did they ask?" Silence

" Shit! That goddamn Maggie and that fucking insurance company. Okay listen you did great sweetie now I'm betting that bitch is on her way over here so I gotta stick around." Yea, Julie's sleeping, dead to the world. I'll go ahead and call you if we have to change plans And honey we have nothing to worry about and after tomorrow night it's over. So just relax and I'll talk to you in a few."

"Love you too honey."

 Laurie stopped the tape and told JR that that was the first call from what she thinks is Sandra, now next comes Kristen about 35 minutes later. Finding the spot where the next phone call came in Laurie let it start.

"Hi Honey." Silence

"Yes,I know. I just had a visit also and so did your sister. I told you that it might happen." Silence

"Would you relax? Their idiots, trust me. They have nothing. They're digging for anything and we're not going to keep going on with this shit." Silence "I agree. Just hang in there one more day and do your part." Silence "I know it's not what we had planned but it's time. We've gone through the scenario at least a hundred times and it's foolproof. Just hang one more day sweetie and come Sunday we're home free. Don't lose it now" Silence. "That's right. I'll text you tomorrow and give you a time. And Honey relax. Nothing is going to go wrong. Everything will go perfectly." Silence. " It will sweetie. Trust me. Love you too."

   With the phone call over, Laurie shut off the recorder and said, "We'll JR, what do you think?"

   " I think you two are the masters and I bow to you. Great work everyone. And I really mean that. You too Sam."

   " Are we done for tonight? I'm thinking of a couple of games of 9 ball to kick Doctor Death's ass there and I can buy that new GPS system for the boat."

   Dr. Death just laughed and said, "Sam, I'm going to take a chance and say I have $20.00 that I will whip your ass."

   JR agreed. "Yeah Sam. Let's call it a night, unless someone has something to add that can't wait till tomorrow, let's say 7 - 8 for breakfast?"

   Maggie just sat there taking everything in and wondering what the hell was going on again. She knew she was new to this kind of investigation but come on, do something. She was at the point of saying that to everyone when JR asked her to take a walk. Grabbing a beer and handing Maggie one without asking her, they walked to the back yard by Sam's and Rita's boat with GD dog following. As the two got close to the water JR asked Maggie what they should do? Maggie had time to cool down but still was pissed.

   "Damn JR. You got to contact someone. Julie's mom and her sister sounded like they were going to be doing something tomorrow night. JR was looking at the sky and said, "And tell them what?" Maggie was getting more pissed as she said,"That you have a recording where Mom and her daughters are going to do something tomorrow night."

   "What recording?"

   "The one we just listened to ! Damn JR, someones gotta listen!"

   "The tapes that were obtained illegally? That could send us to jail for taping illegally? The tapes that were destroyed?" JR said it all in such a mellow tone that she wondered why. Maggie was dumb founded and her face gave that expression as the kid off that movie Home Alone with him shaving and putting aftershave on his face.

   "God dammit JR, I've really had enough of this shit. What the hell am I doing here? And what the hell are you going to do?"

   JR couldn't keep the smile off his face when he asked Maggie if she really thought that anyone at S and W would let harm come to anyone?

   "No I didn't think so but what the hell are you doing about it?" Maggie wasn't prepared for the answer she was to receive,

   "I agree we should do something. You deal with it."

   "Me? You want me to deal with this? I'm calling the police and have them talk to the mother and find out what the hell is going on."

   JR just smiled that damn smile and said, "Maggie, if you think that's the best way then we are behind you 100 percent. Nothings going to happen tonight so if you wake up tomorrow morning and decide that's what you want to do, I'll drive you to the police station and you can tell them." Maggie was not prepared for that answer.

"Really?" Maggie was amazed.

"Of course, we work for you and your company. All I'm asking is that you sleep on it, which I'm going to do. Ready GD Dog?" GD wagged his tail in anticipation of having some alone time with dad and mom and knowing every night he was given a doggie treat that he loved like Sam loved his beer.

As JR walked away he turned to Maggie. "I almost forgot, you may want to call your boss and Mr. Gant and let them know they will be receiving a phone call from Julie's mom if they haven't already. She'll be stating to them that S and W along with you are harassing her poor, helpless, grieving daughter. See you in the morning."

Maggie wasn't in the mood when Jimmy came to bed later that night for anything other than her lover to hold her. Maggie told Jimmy what JR had said about it was up to her to decide what should be done. Jimmy kissed her and told her that whatever she decided to do he was behind her 100 percent and fell asleep almost immediately. Maggie was laying there thinking she would never fall asleep when the next thing she knew it was 6:00 in the morning.She woke with the same thoughts as she had when she fell asleep. Do I call the police? Call her boss and ask him? Wake Jimmy up and ask him? In the end she decided to go downstairs and just to sit for a few and relax by the water and watch the sun come up. Surprised to find Sam up and awake and getting the grill going she asked him if he ever slept.

"Enjoy everyday like it's your last. Plenty of time to sleep when I'm dead. I'll even get you a cup of coffee. Now you look like a poor lost soul so sit

down and enjoy a beautiful morning, I'll even be quiet." Maggie sat there and enjoyed the peace and tranquility that only a morning in Florida can bring and as Sam brought her coffee said that she had to make a decision on calling the police or something happening to Julie. Sam never said a word but just listened. "Sam I know what the right thing to do is to call the police but something is telling me that's something not right. What the hell? Why did you guys let me listen to that tape? It was then that Maggie noticed Rita stepping onto the dock from the boat. "You sleep in there?" Maggie asked Sam.

Sam seemed puzzled. "Of course we do. Best nights sleep you'll ever get with the water swaying you to sleep and the one you love in your arms. It's beautiful. You and Dr. D should try it."

"I doubt that."

"You never know until you try it. Now what seems to be the issue you're having with your case?" Rita had come up and kissed Sam and took a seat with a cup of coffee looking at Maggie waiting for her answer.

Maggie took a minute. "Well the big question I'm having is why S and W is just taking it nice and casual as if nothings going on that can't wait. These ladies are up to something and it's going to happen soon."

"Yeah, tonight most likely." Rita said it as if she didn't have a care in the world.

Maggie was about to say "Then what the hell are we sitting around for," but at that time GD Dog and Venus came running outside and went behind the bath house out of sight. Maggie just sat there wondering what the hell was going on now with the dogs. A minute later JR came outside carrying a cup of coffee and GD Dog running and jumping in Rita's lap. Venus was running back to go inside. Maggie finally figured the dogs were doing their morning ritual and had finished. Coming up and saying good morning to everyone JR asked Sam how he and Dr. D made out in 9 ball.

"Well I let him win a couple. He's getting much better. I will say that for him. I think he's been taking lessons. I wouldn't trust that guy Maggie."

"That's good?" JR asked Sam..

"Yeah. Damn guy took me for $50.00 so Maggie when you two go out for dinner you better be thinking of me."

Maggie was getting more positive that maybe she should be talking to the authority since no one here really cared when JR asked her how she slept.

"Fine till I woke up and was still trying to figure out what I'm supposed to do. And JR to be honest it seems as if you're not taking this seriously."

JR just smiled at her which made Maggie even more peeved and asked her again, "So what should we do?" Maggie wasn't sure and didn't answer. Rita knew why JR was doing this but couldn't take seeing the anguish he had put Maggie into.

"JR, I think Maggie could use some help so maybe you need to explain what she has to work with."

"I will, but I want her to answer one question. Maggie let's pretend that you just walked into the police station and asked to speak to a detective. He'll ask you what he can do for you. Pretend I'm the detective. What would you say to him?"

Maggie had thought about it and looked straight into JR's eyes and said, "I'd tell him I heard a tape last night that I had access to that recorded message and that I heard three ladies plotting something that is going to happen tonight and I believe the police should be involved." As soon as Maggie said it out loud she knew she had screwed up. Shit! JR playing the part of the detective asked Maggie if she could get a copy of the tape.

"I see where you're going with this, and I see that I would just be making an ass of myself. But damn JR, what the hell are we going to do? We have to let someone know."

"Your right and some things have been put into motion after the meeting last night. I think you'll find it will soothe your nerves. For now I'm going to be honest with you and tell you your biggest mistake. First and foremost you have no idea who S and W is and what these people surrounding you are capable of. We would never let any harm come to anyone and we have resources that we can use to obtain our goals. Some are not quite legal but they work and in the long run we can solve more

cases and save more lives than any police department anywhere. So right now I'm going to take a cup of coffee to my wife and grab a shower. I'm asking you personally to do me a favor. Forget about the police. And I want you to think outside the box. You're coming from a corporate world where everyone wears a suit and tie and the women wear dress clothes and when you have a problem you go to the police. Maggie, this isn't TV. People die every day or go missing or commit a crime that no one can figure out who did it. That's when S and W are called. Now please, go relax and think what you would do if you had the best detectives in the world at your fingertips. And Maggie, you're doing a great job, now go relax. You're running the meeting at 8."

With that said JR stood and started to walk back inside but turned around to tell Sam they would meet at 8 and make his eggs over easy and don't burn them like last time.

"Fuck You JR! Does this look like Denny's?"

Just relax JR had told Maggie. Easier said than done. Going up to "their " room, Maggie found her Jimmy snoring dead to the world. This morning Maggie needed him up and awake and made enough noise as she was preparing her clothes and preparing to jump in the shower to wake him.

"We'll good morning my love. Do you think you could be a little louder? The people on the next block didn't hear you. I sure hope you brought me coffee."

"Fuck you Jimmy. Does this look like Denny's? Now get your butt up and wash my back in the shower and then we are taking a walk. GD dogs coming too." Hell it worked for JR, maybe taking a walk with man's best friend has something to do with relaxing.

Chapter 8

The same folks as last night were gathered around the outside patio table with one new face being added. Maggie had seen tall, good looking guys before but this one here was like a god. Over six feet tall he could be a younger Clint Eastwood with blond hair. Dr. Schipero saw Maggie looking and smiled.

"Honey, don't even think about it. He's Tina's through and through and I hear she carries a switch blade and would cut any woman who fucked with him."

Being introduced, Maggie was surprised to find that Mark was as nice as could be as they made small talk while they waited for Sam to yell 'Come and get it'. Grabbing their breakfast, which was served buffet style, Maggie for the first time was actually feeling relaxed. She even knew what she was going to say to the gang as they finished their breakfast.

JR started the meeting. Thanking Sam for another fine breakfast, and saying his eggs were done to perfection, JR asked the pineapple if everyone was on. Maggie by now was starting to recognize voices and knew it was Phil, the office coordinator, when he replied that everyone was and told Mark that it was nice to have him back.

"Nice to be back. I'll go ahead and send over the data later this afternoon. I will say that it was a very successful trip." Data on a diving trip? Maggie knew there were some things she would never figure out. JR seemed pleased as did the rest of S and W partners whose faces she could see.

"Alrighty then. Let's get this show started. Now I went ahead and asked Maggie here to go ahead and tell us what she wants done but before I do let me explain where we stand. Maggie last night two of our partners monitored Jules' house and everything's fine. And thanks Ken and Patricia. Owe you one." A voice Maggie had never heard said it was like old times and it was their pleasure. "So we know nothing happened last night but tonight I think we're going to be in for a different ride. We still don't know what these ladies are up to but I believe with Maggie's help we're going to

find out." Her help? Maggie wasn't stupid and knew she was being tested but why was the question. These people needed her help like a hole in the head.

"Maggie, what would you like us to do to get this case solved?" JR gave his best innocent look he had. Maggie stood up, which wasn't a whole lot higher then when she was sitting and started speaking making eye contact as she did. Having been in many corporate meetings she knew how to run the show.

"First I'd like to thank everyone for this opportunity and will give it my best shot. The folks here and listening know much more than I do,so any input you can throw my way would be greatly appreciated."

Everyone listening knew Maggie was a natural born leader and a great schmoozer to top it off.

"Let's start with the basics. First and foremost is the reason. The kind of money involved we can almost guarantee is the root of it. Second, we think everyone from the two sisters to Mom is involved. Notice I didn't say Julie because I have a feeling she's just a stooge in all this and after yesterday I'm betting Julie may have limited time on the planet unless we do something. That part I'm smart enough to leave up to JR and the rest of you. Third, we know something is going to happen tonight. We don't know what, or how or when only that something is supposed to happen. Now I am going to ask Michelle something but bear with me."

Looking at Michelle who was on amazon looking at baby clothes she asked her, "Michelle, is there anything that you read about this family that would give us some insight other than what you have told us?"

Michelle, who had little Sam on her lap, closed her eyes and thought back. For almost a full minute she became entranced and finally said she had nothing.

"Thanks Michelle. Now Katie, you have heard everything that's been said about these ladies.. What is your opinion starting with Julie?"

"Julie's the easy one, believe it or not. I have a damn strong feeling her mothers been initiating every move she's made since she was fifteen and her father passed on. Julie seems very dependent on her. Even now. I think

by seeing how she's married older men that were financially stable not once but twice, then I'm thinking mom played a part in these marriages. I mean would you let your daughter marry a guy over twice their age? I wouldn't."

"And Sandra?"

"Sandra is a recluse. She has lived with her mother since she was a teenager and never moved out. We see that she doesn't date or travel or even go out with any friends if she even has any. We just don't know a whole lot about her. She's another one that is dependent on her mother for pretty much everything including companionship."

"And ?"

"That's the one I know less about and I have to speculate that she doesn't like men. Very forceful but by listening to the phone conversation with her mother she is also relying on her for some type of support though not monetary but mentally. I'd bet Mom's her crutch."

"Okay, tell us about Mom."

"Mom ? Oh she is a piece of work. She's the Burger Meister. The one that runs the show. We know she likes money to gamble. We know she rules the flock and we know she's manipulative. What I don't think she has is patience.. I think these accidents have been planned out a long time in advance. Mom just doesn't seem to be the type to one, be that patient, or two, be that intelligent. If you ask me, whoever planned these accidents is patient and very, very smart. I just don't see mom as either."

"Thanks Katie, and I agree. We are dealing with someone who so far has beaten the police, the coroners, the Fire Marshall and even OSHA. If it wasn't for S and W we would never have speculated anything and these ladies would have gotten away with murder. Now this morning JR showed me that going to the police wasn't going to work. And he was right, I come from a world that's pretty much black and white and if you have an issue you call the police. Like someone said, this ain't television land. Also someone told me to think out of the box and you know what, I did. Let's put ourselves in Mom's shoes for a minute. Julie has all this money that mom wants a piece of. Me, if I went through the planning and taking the risk I'd not be happy with a new car or some chump change. I'd want it all. And more. Now let's say this plan has been in the making for years. Everyone has done their part. Now I made a phone call this morning to my boss and found out that Julie's life insurance was a big $250,000. Not a lot to kill for but still something. And JR, you were right. Someone called and complained we were hassling Julie so once again you hit the nail on the head. Lawyers were mentioned. No the big pay out is going to be when they sue my insurance company saying that Julie commited suicide for our involvement driving her to be so depressed in her time of grief. It's perfect. And my boss said he would probably end up settling out of court."

No one there said a word or even looked surprised. They just sat there smiling, even her Jimmy. It hit Maggie then. Everyone had figured it out before she had said anything. How smart were these people?

Looking at JR, Maggie was confused. "What the hells going on JR? Rita? Why did you let me ramble on if you knew what was going to happen? And you Jimmy? You didn't tell me? My god I just made a fool out of myself and you let me? What is wrong with you people?" Maggie felt like running and hiding.

Rita knew what needed to be said. "Maggie, do you trust us? Cause I know you do. We all knew you had it in you and when you started thinking like a private investigator and relaxed and forgot about the police it would come to you. And it did. And don't you go blaming the Doc there. We didn't talk to each other about this or agree to not say a word about it to you. We all were 90 percent sure that's what you would say. We had to see if you had what it took and you did. Everyone here was betting that you would come around and we put our faith in you. You came through like the person we all felt you were. You should feel proud and know that we respect you and love having you here, especially that gentleman to your right."

Everything was happening too fast in Maggie's world.

Rita continued, "Now tonight after we're done with this case, we will get into some things that we will explain that will make this perfectly clear. I'm asking you as a friend to bear with us another day and tonight you will see the picture and have everything explained to you. Then you can ask all the questions you want and we will be there to answer them. But I have a feeling that come tonight you'll have figured them out for yourself. Now for now we have to move on and save your company big money and earn our paychecks."

Maggie was tempted to say screw this and pack her bags but she knew what Rita said was true. She did come around and think clearer after she relaxed and it was right in front of her the entire time but the regular world of police was gone and the world of mother's killing their daughters was now here. For some reason JR and GD Dog had left the meeting, leaving Rita to carry on.

"Okay, Maggie just confirmed what we all pretty much knew. Now the big question is how is Julie going to be murdered to make it appear as a suicide? I have a couple of scenarios but let's start with the basics. We have hanging , which is very hard to make look like a suicide especially when the persons not willing. A gun? Same same.. Jumping off a bridge? No way. Which leaves us with pills. Now Maggie was absolutely correct when she said the family would sue for making Julie so depressed that she couldn't take it anymore. I'm betting the sisters will swear in court that Julie had told them today so don't be surprised when Sandra and Kristen call Julie. Of course she's not going to tell them that or she might be so out of it that mom will answer the phone for her. All they want is a record on file that they called.

And I'm betting the Mother calls again today just so they can say they tried to warn Maggie's company twice about this investigation Maggie is performing and how depressed it's making Julie. It will leave a record and will look good in court. This brings us to the murder itself. We're betting on its pills. Now I think Moms already got her pretty drugged up. With just a few more pills, I'd say Julie is a goner. What's going to be the key to this whole thing is going to be timing. Mom is not going to be there when Julie dies. She's most likely going to be back at home with Sandra as an alibi. Mom already has the suicide note ready to be typed out on Julies computer. The computer and printer have to be Julies or the suicide notes no good. She most likely has it all figured out on what she's going to say and type it right before she leaves. No one is going to know until the minute when Julie dies only that mom was at home picking up clothes or some other bullshit and when she came back to Julies that she was found dead from overdosing. Dr. Shapiro, what would you do if they brought Julie in for an autopsy?"

"Easy, blood work could tell you everything and it would work. The problem I see is we have no idea what shes been drugging her with or if shes going to use the same thing to have her commit suicide with."

"No we don't know but I'm pretty sure someone does. Michelle, you said Sandra worked for Hospice and was let go. Tina you said that you couldn't find any record why. I'd like you to go back on the computer and find us anything, a name of her supervisor's, co-worker, anyone that might have an inkling of what she was let go for. I have an idea that Sandra was let go for pills coming up missing."

Maggie was actually enjoying herself again using a part of her brain that hadn't been used before. Before she knew it she was speaking out loud, "We'd be wasting our time looking for old pills. No, we need to know what Mom's been giving Julie and see what she got planned for tonight's concoction. "

JR and GD Dog were back. "Sam, you want to handle this?" JR asked Sam but everyone noticed JR looked confused. There was something there that didn't quite add up and JR's mind was racing overtime.. Try as he might, he could not get a clear picture.

"Me? You want the old timer cook to help you solve this? The guy who got beat by a rookie in pool games last night and now has to eat peanut butter sandwiches all week because I can't afford food for his poor ailing wife? The guy who someone or someone's made ride in a shitty plane and then a piece of shit compact car? Me?"

Laughing JR knew that Sam had figured out what needed to be done.. Before discussing his plan Sam asked the Doc that if he did an autopsy on Julie and the chemicals came up as fentanyl or some medication that was highly toxic wouldn't he alert the police handling this case?

The Doc said the police always received a copy of the autopsy report. He would definitely highlight the drugs if they were considered illegal. And they would be notified immediately.

Sam said that the ladies should be looking at what Julie had been prescribed in the past.

Sam, when Sam wanted to be, was probably one of the best detectives at S and W, he just played a good game and as he was getting older he wanted the new detectives to use their brain. He then explained to everyone why and what to do regarding Julies suicide.

"First, if these ladies have been planning this for years, then they have had more than enough time to plan out every little detail. They are going to use something that Julie has in her medicine cabinet. And it could be in the second husband's name. I had to have knee surgery once when Rita tripped me getting on the boat. (Rita spoke up and said he had too many beers) and I had more pain pills then I knew what to do with. We ended up throwing most of them away. Christ if I had used all of them I would have been a drug addict. A few years back the doctors gave you anything you wanted plus some. Of course your insurance company paid for them so who cared. What I'm saying is look at Julie's and Jim Bane's past medical history. And Ryans. Good drugs could last 3 years. Ain't that right Tina?"

"Sam, you're an asshole." As Tina said it she was shaking her head smiling. She thought that was a pretty good one coming from Sam.

For the next 15 minutes Sam's plan was discussed. In the end the gang knew that it wasn't foolproof but may just work with a little work. Before discussing the plan Sam had asked Dr. D and Maggie to wait in another room out of ear shot. They were told that they may have to answer questions to the authority and S and W did not want them to lie.

Alone, Maggie asked Jimmy what was going on. Jimmy would have loved to tell her but even he had no idea. All he knew is that if Sam asked for them to wait out of ear shot then somehow they would have a major part to play in tonight's activities.

Sam's plan was not going to be that easy to achieve. His first reasoning is that they needed a camera in Julie's kitchen. They couldn't wait for mom to leave and hope that Julie would be all right. They needed to see her as she was preparing the concoction she would give to Julie which seemed to be in the tea mom had been giving her. Second item on the agenda involved a call from an untraceable cell phone to Maggie and with Dr. Shapiro in attendance would be informed that Julie was being poisoned by her mother. Maggie and Dr.Shapiro would in turn tell JR who would contact the police and call an old friend from the police department who would arrive seconds later to save the day. Sam, who would just happen to be close by, would go in with them and remove the camera and the bug Michelle had planted. Mom would be taken in for questioning. It was at this point they stopped. Maggie and the doc were then asked to come back out to join the conversation.

"Sorry about you two not being here.. I can't say what we discussed. But if you and the Doc would help us out by staying here today, especially after say 6 and if Maggie would make sure her phone was totally charged and near her at all times it would help us in case of any emergencies. Now I'm going to need some input here from everyone. Lets say Mom is taken in for suspicion of trying to kill Julie. She's in jail and has to call someone. My bet is Sandra. Now we know mom is not going to say a word cause right now all they have her on is suspicion of trying to kill Julie. We still can't prove shit. We need to get all three so how do we do it?" No one said a word.

"Sam, let's take a break. We all need another cup of coffee and it will give us time to think. Let's say 20 minutes." Rita agreed with the condition no one was to go shoot any pool. She said that part looking at Sam and Dr. D. As they waited for the meeting to resume Maggie and Jimmy were sitting outside with Thomas and Katie just enjoying the coolness of a July morning before the heat came back in full force later in the day. Maggie had put the morning's trial and errors to the side. It was sometimes hard for her to grasp that they were working a murder case and she was involved. Katie out of the blue asked Maggie what her and the Docs plans were for the future. They had been dating for over two years and wondered how she knew. Then she thought back to what Jimmy had said about S and W knowing more about her then he did and let it go. Maggie went on to tell Katie that soon she would be retiring and so would Jimmy and though they knew they wanted to be together they just couldn't figure out the final chapter in their lives. Maggie found herself opening up to Katie and the two sat there and talked as two old friends. Without realizing it the 20 minutes went by as if just a few minutes had passed. Everyone was back and settling back in when Sam asked if anyone had a solution. It was Rita this time who spoke up. "Sam, you can forget about Mom. She's not all that bright but she's smart enough to keep her mouth shut until she talks to Sandra."

"Sandra? What about Kristen?"

"Forget about Kristen for now. My moneys on Sandra being the brains and Kristen's in it for the money and to get a chance to help kill men who remind her of her father."

"Keep going." Sam was impressed.

"Let's assume that Daddy had a thing for teenage girls. Let's also assume that Julie being the youngest was not affected by Daddy's love and tenderness, yet. That would explain a lot. Now let's go with maybe Mom knew what was happening or found out after Daddy's accidental death. Maybe Mom looked the other way or maybe it was said jokingly that they would be better off with daddy gone. We may never know. All we do know is something tied them together in a murderous plot that involved accidental deaths. Kristen was gone shortly afterwards but kept in touch with mom. I'm betting Kristen wanted a piece of the pie and knew what was happening and was happy it was Julie and not her that the two had chosen. Now we know Sandra is a recluse but she has to be getting her information somewhere. I went ahead and map quested her house in location to the nearest library. It's only a ten minute walk."

"JR, why is it that me and my wife have to do everything around here? I want a raise. Go on honey, show them what else you know."

JR just smiled and nodded 'Yes'. He never said a word about the feeling of doubt he was having. Something just felt off. It reminded JR of bowling when you threw that perfect strike ball but as soon as you released the ball you knew it was going to be a split

Rita continued, "That's it Sam. That's just my opinion now you clowns figure out what to do."

"Thanks honey, now I know why I married you." Shaking her head Rita said she still couldn't understand why she married him.

Tina, who was always the quiet one, said she agreed with Rita and that the only way to get all three were to use one against the other.

Sam was looking at JR smiling. "I agree with Tina and thank you. Damn JR, these ladies are making you look like a LOSER! Maggie, your turn, what have you got?"

"I too agree with Rita and Tina especially where Tina said you have to play one against the other. My bet is Sandra's is never going to break. We should be concentrating on Kristen and playing her against the Mom. After the suicide attempt, I'd try and keep Sandra from talking to those two as much as possible."

"Anyone disagree or have a different opinion?" No one said a word. "All right JR, we solved it and even told you what to do. You think you can figure out how to do the rest without the ladies and my help?" Sam was grinning ear to ear.

JR was pleased, especially with Tina. She was finally coming out of her shell slowly but she was coming along. "Great work you guys and unfortunately I am going to need everyone's help. First, as Sam said, forget about Hospice and the meds. We can't be 100 percent sure if we find Sandra stole will even be used. Now I or Sam can probably talk to our friend in the police department to prolong the phone calls as long as possible but by law Mom has to be able to call someone at some point. They have to abide by the law so the most we can hope for is an hour or maybe two. It would be a shame if Sandra's phone was turned off for say three hours tonight wouldn't it Tina?" Tina just smiled.

"Now comes the fun part. Someones going to have to be there to talk to Kristen when Mom gets arrested to tell her that her Mom was arrested for trying to kill Julie and is singing like a songbird about how she and Sandra were responsible. And Sandra is nowhere to be found and $50,000 dollars is missing from Julie's account. What do you think 's first response would be?"

Thomas just said, "Call Sandra."

"Right. And Sandra's not answering because her phone is disconnected. Next Kristen is going to try calling her mom's cell phone is what I'm thinking. What I'm suggesting is we take Mom's cell phone and talk to Kristen . That's when we tell her some bullshit about her mom saying she was just doing it because she and her sister threatened her or some bullshit like that. We tell her that a police officer should be there any moment and for her to stay put till they do. We will know that one of us is already there talking to Kristen but this will make it perfectly clear that this ain't no game. What this calls for is a motherly figure. So Rita wants to take a trip with Sam and Thomas this afternoon to Jacksonville? I'd like Katie to go also for a backup for Rita when she's talking to Kristen ." Sam and Thomas were stunned.

Thomas wasn't happy. "No way JR! It was hell on me last time. And I can't take Sam's bitching any more!" JR needed Sam here to deal with the police anyway but he knew it would get Thomas's goat.

"All right, Sam's staying but I need you there since you know the area but the jet is back and I'm sure Tina will make sure you get a luxury car to drive. That's okay then? And Katie's going with you if that's okay.? Rita, I think Katie can handle Kristen."

"As long as I don't have to listen to Sam's bitching it's fine. And I'd Love to spend some time with my wife. We need a romantic weekend."

Sam was pissed. "What? He's getting the jet and a luxury car? Tina I swear if I find your involved in that last trip to Jacksonville you're definitely out of my will. And you and Casanova there can't call your first born Lil Sammy the second! I mean it!"

Rita, as she gave Tina a wink said for the umpteenth time, "Sam, would you relax? Tina has said again and again that she had nothing to do with that trip. It was just fate."

"Fate my ass!!"

"Moving on. Maggie you will be here with Doc, Tina, Tim, Laurie and Michelle helping to make sure everything goes like clockwork and to help out as needed. Everyone's going to be wearing mics and earpieces so let's keep the chatter down to a minimum."

Sam I need you to call our good friend at the police dept. and get everything ready for tonight. You and I will be there waiting for Laurie's call at Julies tonight. For now Michelle I need you Maggie and Rita to visit Julie's house and see if Mom will let them in so you can place a camera in the kitchen."

Maggie had a question. "Excuse me JR, but if it's like last time Mom's going to make us stay just inside the front door. Even with Michelle pretending to use the bathroom it won't get us in the kitchen."

JR smiled. "Oh, I forgot. Myself, Casanova and GD Dog, our trained flammable liquids sniffing canine, are going to be arriving 5 minutes after the ladies. I promised GD Dog that he could come so he's going to earn his pay. Casanova, aka Mark, is going to knock on the door and let Mom know we needed one more look in the back to finish up. Trust me, I'm betting Moms going to have no problem wanting to see what's going on outside of the kitchen window and what we're up to. Thomas, you and Katie need to leave now and let us know when you get there. Tim, could you set these two up with a hardware bag? Make sure the recorder has plenty of power."

Chapter 8

 By the time the ladies got to Julie's house it was almost noon and getting hotter every minute. Stepping out of the air conditioned van made Maggie feel like she was stepping into a furnace.

   Mark had asked JR what he was supposed to do when they got there. "It's easy. We're going to wait in the Van and when Michelle starts coughing you're going to start making your way up to the door and then we're going to give them a couple of minutes to follow mom into the kitchen then you'll go to the front door and knock loudly. Me and GD Dog will be making our way to the back. This way Mom comes to see who's at the front door and gives Michelle time to set the camera.."

   JR gave the ladies time to maneuver their way inside and it appeared by listening to Mom she was none too happy to see them. Walking to the back JR could hear Mom saying that Julie had gone back to bed and that she was starting to get worried that the investigation on top of her husband dying was really taking too much of a toll on her spirits. Maggie told her she was just doing her job. It was then Michelle started coughing. Slowly at first then a little heavier. Asking for a glass of water Mom said to the ladies to follow her. She wasn't letting anyone out of her sight.

   It was at that time that as Mark was almost to the front door that it hit JR like a ton of bricks. Damn how could he have been so supid. Everything that had him feeling they were missing something came into perfect view.

   JR quickly said into his microphone loudly, "Abort, I'm saying abort. Michelle, do not set that camera! Everyone listen, make up some excuse and you ladies leave. Make up some excuse and leave quickly. Tell Mom that one of S and W's detectives was just involved in an accident or any bullshit but just leave soon. No more questions for Mom. But there is one more tricky part and Mark listen up. Michelle or Rita, you need to get that bug out from underneath that end table that Rita set when you went to the bathroom last time. What I need you to do Michelle is say "I hope Mr. Kay will be alright. At that time Mark will knock on the front door. You three by then should just be entering the living room. You will know when the time is right.

   Maggie as you three leave, apologize and tell Mom you will call her tomorrow to set an appointment when Julie is available. Phil, get a hold of Thomas and Katie and tell them to turn around. We will meet back at the house and I'll explain everything. All right, let's get it done and get home. I'll explain everything then. Tina please stand by the computer. I'll be calling you very soon."

   It was an hour before Mark pulled the van into the garage. Seeing that everyone was there who was supposed to be there gave JR a sense of pride knowing that these were some of the smartest people in the field. And they had almost lost everything.

Once inside JR found everyone sitting or standing around the dining room table looking at him and waiting for answers. Maggie especially.

GD Dog came in following JR and went outside. He had hoped for more excitement. All he got was a stupid ride and a very small walk. He was hoping JR forgot his poop bags when they went for their walk. He decided to start saving up.

Sam didn't hesitate. "JR you got 30 seconds to tell us what's going on or I'm taking you outside and putting frozen fish in your pants, tying you hand and legs together and throwing you in the water!

JR could always count on Sam for a stupid quote.

"Sam we almost screwed up big-time. And let me tell you why: We assumed. And what did we assume? We assumed that what we heard going on at Julies house was true and that good ole mom was going to kill Julie tonight and make it look like suicide. We assumed that the answers that were given to us by the daughters were true or not true depending on how they played it. This pointed all of us in the direction they wanted us to go. They've been leading us this whole time."

Maggie had been waiting for an answer and this was not the one she was hoping for.

"Excuse me JR but what would be the point?" someone asked.

JR just waited and looked at everyone, waiting for an answer.

Rita figured it out first. "They were using us to protect themselves. Damn that's smart."

JR could see a couple of people were still trying to figure it out.

"Rita hit it right on the nose! Let's say we went ahead with this plan. Tonight we are watching the camera and see Mom mix up a cup of tea with what we assume is the suicide pills. So now we're getting ready to interview the sisters and do our pretend call to Maggie and the Doc and the police go in. I would bet you a hundred dollars they would have to break the door down because Julie is not going to answer the door because she took a couple of sleeping pills to help her sleep and probably has one of those headsets on to play relaxing music or some crap that's supposed to make you sleep.

So now you have the police that just destroyed the door and breaking and entering standing there looking like idiots and you have us looking like bigger idiots. It would have been quite a show. And this show would have been just starting. Julie wakes up and asks what the hell is going on. She's hysterical and calls her Mom who just happened to be running out for some milk or whatever. Returning Mom says thank god she had someone install hidden cameras in Julie's house. She was worried about Julies and her safety of course, so she played back the tape from the hidden security cameras while the police were still there. Lo and behold are our tickets to the unemployment line. Oh, no worries, Maggie would have been there with us all along. She also would be standing in line for food stamps with the rest of us."

Rita asked if JR was 100 percent sure of his scenario and who's to say that Mom really wasn't out to kill Julie?

"Rita, from the beginning everyone agreed that these ladies were intelligent. Someone even said they were Michelle smart if they commited these murders. And I agree. That's what was nagging me. Yesterday we heard Mom talk to both of the daughters. Or did we?"

JR again waited while everyone let it soak in.

Rita couldn't believe it. "You're saying there was no one on the other end? But we heard it ring and she was talking to them."

"Did we? I called and asked Tina to check phone records for yesterday. No calls were made to Julie's n or out. None of the daughter's cell phones show a call placed to Julie's home phone. They knew we w et up a listening device and played it. Just like today they knew we would try and set a camera. Now omething has been bothering me about this case since I woke up this morning and I just couldn't figure out. Then it came to me. Why would Mom and the daughters be talking about what was going to happe onight on the phone? And yes I know they never came out and said that they were going to kill Julie to but the innuendo was there, and let's think back to Michelle going to the bathroom. Mom didn't need t n the hallway watching her. Mom would have locked the doors to bedrooms or whatever you didn't wa adies going into or taking a peek. We assumed Mom was being cautious but what she was doing was allowing Rita to set a bug. We almost screwed ourselves by underestimating these ladies. We forgot tha had years to plan this and they knew that a Five star detective agency would probably set a bug. And it' of the best laid plans that should have worked and I hate to admit it but whoever is the brains behind th could have been a hell of a detective. Instead of a psychopath. Phil, how bad could they have made this

Phil hesitated before speaking. "JR, I hate to admit it but these ladies are very smart or at least one or two of them are, and they did think of everything and knew what we were going to do before we did. Now what we have to ask ourselves is why are they doing this? They knew these were the perfect accidents. You even said we couldn't prove a damn thing. So Maggie's company and Mr. Gant's company have to pay out eventually. No, what these ladies want is to set back and forget about it and make some more money. And they did it perfectly. Now we have Facebook, Twitter, and countless other social media sites they could have posted this poor helpless woman getting fucked over by the police, S and W and the insurance companys and they have video to show and god knows they would be showing it. And trust me, this is ready to go once this would have happened. They have a lawyer I'm betting just waiting. There is another way they could play it and that's to settle out of court. And to be honest S and W probably would have gone that way. And it wouldn't be cheap. So as you said JR, these ladies are killing two birds with one stone. No other detective agency would take this case after S and W was made a fool out of and I'm betting Mr. Gant and Mr. Wood would just pay Julie and be done with it wishing they had never hired S and W. Either way the ladies come out smelling like a rose.

For only the second time in history a pin falling in that dining room could have been heard.

Maggie was sitting there trying to absorb this information when JR continued by talking into the speaker phone.

"Mr. Wood, you've been in the insurance business for years, have you ever heard of anything like this?"

Maggie had no idea Mr. Wood was listening in and was glad she hadn't used any foul language. She would have to thank Sam afterwards.

"Never. And I hope never to hear of another one like this. We get insurance scams all the time but not to this degree. What's worse is it probably would have worked. If the death certificate says accidental death then we have to pay. And that's not counting the money we'd be sued for. JR I want you to solve this case, and I won't lie to you. It's about the money. Now I want it to be about taking those bitches for everything we can. Phil and I were speaking beforehand and told me Julie has property worth a couple of million. And if S and W can prove these weren't accidents you're getting a hell of a bonus compliments from Julie. So FUCK her and her family. I'm tired of these assholes trying to fuck me over."

Maggie had never heard Mr. Wood say one curse word in over 30 years besides damn and hell.

JR actually laughed. "Mr. Wood, we're halfway there. We know now that Mom and Julia are in on it. The two sisters I'd bet are playing a big part also. Our problem was we underestimated them. That won't happen again. I'll ask Maggie to give you a call later . Right now we're going to talk to a guy who might shed some light on this ladder situation . But before I let you go I have a question for you. Actually it is for you and Phil."

"Phil, you filled out the contract and sent it to who at Harvest Salt?"

" I sent one copy only to the financial manager. He signed and Mr. Wood and Mr. Gant signed. They sent it back and I had Casanova pick up a hard copy."

Mr. Wood was not stupid. "I see where you're going with this. Besides myself and the financial manager no one has access to our computer."

Maggie spoke up. "JR, you're thinking someone knew it was the S and W agency that would be handling this case.? That's easy. We have a board where everyone knows where you're at and someone updates daily."

"Yes, but that wouldn't give them much time and I have a feeling someone was watching as soon as you landed. Anyways not much we can do about it now. Mr. Wood when you talk to Mr. Gant, mention it to him and see if he has any thoughts on this matter.

Everyone had more questions as Katie asked JR to take a walk with her. Telling everyone to relax but not go too far the two were back in 10 minutes. It was then that JR gave his plan.

"Our last plan almost cost us our business and this time we're going to seal those ladies' fate one way or another. Now let's use what we know about them so far. First their patient. This last plan of theirs almost worked to the tee. That took months if not years of planning. We got lucky. I'm not sure any other detective agency would have. Now my question to you folks was this their only plan? I believe it was. Sam, your opinion?

"Hell JR, if it wasn't for you figuring out what was happening I would be living in a little row boat now. And Rita would have to go back to work. And her days of being a stripper are almost over so we might be living on minimum wage. Seems to me their goal was to harm the detective agency, whether it was ours or someone else and the insurance companies. I also don't believe any other detective agency would have put a bug in their house to hear what they were saying. Most would have just charged the insurance company big money for a couple of days work and said that they were accidents. This plan was reserved for a company like ours. So as far as another plan, they will have to come up with something fast."

JR asked if everyone agreed.

Unanimous yes.

" Now next we know they are smart. And one of them is a geek and knows hardware and computers or they have someone there paying that is, which I doubt. These ladies are smart enough to keep it all in the family I have a feeling. The only way we will find out this information is on the computer and phone calls and going back to everything the two accidents have to offer. Which brings me to the next point. From this moment on every lady is Katie Rodriquez when they're dealing with someone on the phone or in person. We want the name Katie Rodriguez to get back to everyone in that screwed up family. Find out who their beauticians are, their drycleaners, their neighbors, anyone and everyone that might have had contact before or after the accidents .. Just make sure you say you're Katie."

Thomas was pretty sure that's what Katie wanted to talk to JR about when she wanted to go for a walk. Using herself as a target.

JR saw Thomas's concern and told the group that for the next few days Thomas and Cassonova would be in charge of Katie's security.

"Next is Tim and Laurie. You get a delightful afternoon checking the vans for tracers and walking around this property and adjoining property for cameras and if you find one or more, leave them. And be discreet. Use the high powered binoculars and an upstairs window but don't let them know we know about any cameras they may have. We will disconnect them later after the show."

Sam of course volunteered for this duty asking what show?

"No Sam, I have something important for you, Thomas and Cassanova have nothing to do since Katie doesn't need security yet so you guys are going to go get a thirty foot ladder and a list of everything the first husband was wearing including the caulk, rag and everything else the man had on him. Also pool floaties like the little kids wear."

" Pool Floaties? What the hell do we need pool Floaties for?" Sam was curious and didn't like where this was headed.

" I wouldn't want to go up on that ladder and get pulled over without some protection. I also need you guys to pick up a cheap mattress so you have something soft to land on."

" What the fuck are you talking about JR? I ain't going nowhere near that ladder!"

"Then it has to be Thomas. Thomas, don't forget the pool floaties or mattress."

Thomas was staring wide eyed. "JR forget it. No way am I doing that!"

"All right, let's ask the Doc. Doctor D who would most resemble in size to husband number 1? Sam or Thomas?"

Sam asked why it couldn't be Casanova?.

"Sam, you know Casanova wants kids. You expect us to send a young man up 30 feet and have him get pulled over and break something he might need later. Shame on you."

Thomas and Sam were silent when JR looked at the Doc and said, "All right, screw it. Let's just give Laurie's Dad a call in Jacksonville and see if has any real men working ."

Sam and Thomas knew they had been played. Even Casanova walked by them laughing.. It appeared as if even GD Dog had a smile on his face.

JR stopped everyone. "Hold on everyone. Right now Mom I'm betting knows we pulled the bug cause she just happened to casually check the cameras and she wants to see if she missed anything in the kitchen.. Laurie, what is she going to do?"

Laurie gave it a minute. "She's freaking right now. Did the ladies plant one in the kitchen ? She can't be too obvious because she's going to show this tape to the police. It's not going to look good if she tears up everything to find a camera. So right now she and Julie are reviewing her cameras in the kitchen with the computers in Julie's bedroom I bet with the security cameras on it. They're going to spend a lot of time and still not be 100% sure. So they're going to wait for tonight and see if the police show up. As far as having the tape that show's Rita setting a bug there is no proof. Rita could just say it was gum. They have nothing."

JR told everyone, "And the police will show up. The one officer is going to show up, knock on the front door, receive no answer and leave. What are the ladies going to do?"

No answer for a good twenty seconds and it was Michelle who answered with a big smile on her face. " Honey, better yet, play this back at them. They have no idea we, meaning you figured this out. Have Lieutenant Dan pull up with his light flashing into Julie's driveway about five minutes after Mom has left, he gets out, knocks a couple of times and leaves. If the timing is right Mom has been called by Jule to say that the police were here but there's just one and he knocked on the door and looks like he's leaving. Have Lieutenant Dan leave his business card. Now the next step is actually going to be fun. Now Julie is supposed to be sound asleep and or dying. So she can't go to the front door to retrieve the lieutenant's card to see what this is about and why no one entered so mom has to come back. Now calling the lieutenant, that's when the fun really starts. The scenarios are endless, but no matter what happens the blame is off S and W and put on the police dept.. Make sure you have Lieutenant Dan tape everything. Maggie, you're going to like Lieutenant Dan. Everyone does. He's always over here playing poker with the guys and his wife is so tiny and sweet and we drink Margaritas or sometimes we call it a girl's night and......

Rita again, "Sweetie?"

"Right. So anyways it shows that S and W tried so it buys us more time. That's what you wanted, honey?"

If there was a word stronger than true love JR felt it. "Yes dear."

JR went over what everyone was supposed to do and took Rita aside and told her to keep an eye on Sam and the guys Rita had a feeling JR knew about the cell phone tracker. Next JR grabbed Michelle and GD and took a leisurely walk to nowhere. Just a walk to relax. Today JR had a request.

"Honey, you know I'm halfway intelligent but today I need your help. I can't figure out how a lady could push over a 30 foot ladder by herself, leaving no marks or evidence."

Michelle stopped and looked at JR and holding his face in both hands said, "Leverage sweetie."

"Honey I know that."

"Love of my life, you think I can just go on line and look up how to push a man over on a 30 foot ladder? Without leaving any evidence? It uses leverage but no one has written that certain chapter yet. Whoever did this did it the old fashioned way. Trial error and knew the concept of leverage. Just as you do. Now would you please get this case solved, I'd think everyone at S and W needs a weekend in the Keys.

This was a point JR thought was too good to be true. There had to be two ladders and a place to insure this worked. He was going to use his house to practice on. Where had the culprit found a place to figure out the correct leverage...

JR used his cell and called Phil and asked him to call Laurie's Dad, the painting contractor in Jacksonville and see if he could bring a 30 foot ladder and a couple of guys down here tomorrow morning. "Give him just the basic info on what we're trying to prove. Also he might have to do some touch up painting on the house afterwards. Let me know what he says asap cause if not we're going to have to get someone else, but I like to use him if you agree. There's no way I'm sending anyone up on that ladder who aint a pro."

Phil laughed and agreed. He also reminded JR that Peter Belkins was flying in tomorrow at eleven to interview and he and Maggie, Rita and Sam were supposed to meet him.

 Shit, JR had forgotten.

Phil knew JR's mind had put this on the back burner. "Don't worry, Ritas got a luncheon at your place planned at noon. Everyone who has time from S and W's is going to be there to meet him, but from what Casanova said we're going to like this guy."

"How did he check out?

Phil laughed again, " JR, going by his record he could be Tina's long lost uncle. No wonder she recommended him. Also I'm supposed to tell you that it's not her responsibility to talk to Maggie. I'm assuming you haven't?" Phil knew he hadn't.

 "In case you haven't noticed I've been kind of busy. But I'll do that as soon as I go back. Shit!."

 "Just a suggestion, but why not have Tina and Cassanova take her and the Doc out for dinner and talk to her? And tell them to make it someplace fancy."

 JR knew what Phil was saying without actually saying it.

 "Phil, do me a favor and text everyone and let them know we are having a change of plans. We will meet by the pool in 20 minutes and just relax till then. And it's going to be a very quick meeting."

 Meetings as meetings did not go as JR planned. Starting by saying that Phil was contacting Laurie's Dad who was a major painting contractor in Jacksonville, who had painted the house they now lived in. He was going to let them know as soon as he had an answer. Laurie spoke up and said her father would be down here by 11 - 11:30 with ladders and a couple of real men (Sam and Thomas did not find that amusing the second time it was said to them).

Next he asked if Maggie and Doc would like to have a fancy night out with Tina and Cassanove?..... Aka Mark. He had to stop calling him Casanova.

 JR saw Rita give a smirk and knew right away she knew something he didn't.

 Doctor D told JR that he was cooking his grandmother's steamed shrimp with rice and beans for everyone tonight. Tina spoke up and said after a quick dinner she and David were turning off their phones and a "Do not Disturb" sign would be on their door. And she said it looking JR directly in the eyes.

 "Okay, I tried."

Sam said he and Rita would love a night out.

JR just looked at Sam telling him NO!

Rita had to leave the room before she burst out in laughter.

"All right, moving right along we have a gentleman named Peter coming here for a luncheon tomorrow so everyone can meet him. Phil said that he checked out so let's see. He is supposed to be a wizard on the computer and Tina and Mark speak highly of him. "

"Next is this case. We now realize that whoever did this is as we said patient. And thorough. Let's think for just a minute that whoever made that ladder fall just didn't figure the leverage out on a piece of paper. How would they make sure it worked?"

Mark, who hadn't said much at all, said, "Someone would have to try it first".

"That's right, they would experiment first. Let's move on to the second death. Husband blows himself up. How did the killer know how much acetylene to escape in that size room without blowing up the house? I'm sure there are some principals out there on how much acetylene is needed to ignite in a closed environment but lets just assume that they did this half assed. What could be the outcome?

The first husband just twisted his ankle and got up and the killer had to run like hell or shoot him, which throws out the whole insurance scam. And husband number 2? He's just permanently maimed, crippled and Julie spends the rest of her life taking care of an invilid.

"Katie, you're the expert on psychos. What's your gut saying?"

Katie didn't answer right away. When she did it was a question. "How exactly did Julie and Ryan meet or Julie and Jim Bane?"

JR had no idea and no one in listening distance did either.

"Is that important?"

Katie still did not answer right away. "JR, I know where you're going with this. This killer was meticulous and knew that Husband #1 would be on the ladder and that it would fall and fast. Also that husband #2 would be alleviated along with everything else but not touch the house. So practice makes perfect and the killer experimented beforehand. Right?"

"As far as I can see, one of them had to."

"From what we know so far from the documentation of Julie is that she wasn't a bar slut. So how did she meet a guy older than her and was a roofer and drank a lot? I'm betting it was on an online dating service. So getting back to the original question, was this accident practiced beforehand? The answer is yes and Ryan was hand selected either through Julie or a family member. The same with husband #2. So here's what I think: These ladies had the accidents planned and perfected before the husbands became husbands. Now we all at one time went on an online dating app.. For guys it's different then women a little bit but Julie in her profile could pretty much have an unlimited search for guys, especially if she wrote that she liked older guys and included a seductive picture of herself. So what I'm saying is that you have no idea where and when this property or place you're looking for is or when they used it. They could have rented a place years ago, used it, and moved on. There's a thousand different possibilities from ten years ago till three years ago when the first husband died.

That's all JR needed to hear. "Thanks Katie. I think we'll call it a day. Maggie, I'd like for you to take a ride over to Jim's Roofing and talk to Ryan's boss, who is also the owner, if I can squeeze you away from the doc there. The rest of you I'll see you at dinner for some of Doc's shrimp. But if you ladies decide you want to look something up on the computer, find us a property the sisters used for experimenting. And another thing, these ladies if they're that smart have a computer set up someplace along with an answering machine.

Chapter 10

Looking at Michelle he said he loved her and 'see ya soon' and grabbed GD Dog and headed to a van. Looking back at Maggie he asked if she was coming along?

Maggie had not the slightest idea what the hell was going on. Everything was moving fast then slow then faster. Once in the van seated next to GD dog who jumped on her lap looking out the window she basically said so.

"You really dont think there's anything we should be doing now besides going over and talking to Ryan's boss?"

"Yes, at least a hundred different things."

Maggie had not expected that answer.

JR continued. "A good business is based on common sense and knowing people. This case has been twisted and turned and everyone is trying to get their head around it. These bitchs are smart and one thing we need right now is clear heads, You're not going to do that by making everyone keep thinking. ...give them some R and R or at least tell them to relax a little bit and you'll get twice as much out of them. These detectectives are so smart they make me look like a simpleton. I just got lucky. What you want is detectives to think out of the box. We underestimated these ladies. We got so used to dealing with everyday criminals who almost always make a mistake that when one of these cases were dealing with actual above intelligent criminals we have a hard time adjusting to the fact that anyone could be that smart. "

JR gave Maggie a minute to let that soak in before asking her if she ever sat in a meeting that she didn't need to be in?

Maggie had.

"Now I'm betting Mark and Tina were not 100 percent focused. Their thinking about tonight and with Mark being gone for the last couple of weeks, I don't blame them. Even your Doctor D. He's looking to make a great impression tonight for you cooking. And Rita's got a luncheon she's planning for tomorrow praying that Sam is on his best behavior.

What I learned from Rita and Sam is that meetings are a necessary evil. You keep them short and casual. All the detectives at S and W have two unwritten goals. The first being to enjoy life and family. The second is money. Every case that S and W takes on is based on money, Barbara and Phil are the two that decide what cases we take. Before them it was Sam and Rita, Before them it was another couple, and so on and so on back to the 1930's when S and W was started. The original owners of S and W were ahead of their time. We have no employee of the month, no letters of appreciation because everyone here at S and W is equal. There's no infighting or trying to make yourself look good by making someone else look bad or being worried about losing your job. Now times have changed since the

1930's. We have more social media than we can handle. We have fake news, real news and anyone else who wants to put their two cents in. At S and W we just live each day as if it's our last. We try to enjoy life while doing the best job we can. We don't talk about politics, religion or any personal views that could upset anyone. Our goal is the case which we are working on and enjoying life and making S and W money.

Sitting there listening to JR, Maggie was enjoying the history lesson and how much it made sense.

"Maggie, has Doc said anything about relocating to Delaware when he retires?"

Telling JR that of course they had, she just wasn't sure he'd like it.

"It gets cold as shit some winters."

Laughing, JR told her he was sure those two would figure out some way to keep warm.

"Maggie what would you say if I told you we were opening up a new second office in Delaware? And that we at S and W would like for you and Doc to go to work as two new detectives and help set up everything? Before answering let me say Thomas and Katie would be there as well. Also the computer guy we're meeting tomorrow, if everyone agrees, would also be working there. Along with a couple of new detectives were looking at. So take tonight and think about it. Talk to your sweetie, and anyone else you'd like to. Don't say anything now but take today and tonight and think about it and give me an answer tomorrow. And Phil has already talked to Mr. Wood and he agrees that you have more potential than you're using."

"JR, what the hell. I've never shot a gun and I know absolutely nothing about being a detective, so why the hell would you want me?"

JR took his eyes off the road for just a second and looked at Maggie, "You have something we need. Intelligence and best of all, you think outside the box."

Maggie had no idea what to say. She needed to talk to Doc.

Pulling into the parking lot of Jim's Roofing it was exactly as Maggie pictured it, Small parking lot in front for customers and bigger in the back for the employees parking and their business vehicles. Not many customers came into a roofing showroom.

Parking, JR let GD Dog out and Maggie watched as the dog ran to a shaded place on the sidewalk and waited for the two.

Maggie asked JR if dogs were allowed inside?

"We're going to find out. Let me give you a secret I learned. We're going into a roofing contractors showroom. It's nothing fancy. Now if the owner is a dog lover he would love to have a GD Dog visit. If he doesn't like dogs then the receptionist will tell us "No Dogs allowed" and probably point to a sign and at which point I'll bring GD Dog back to the van, turn the AC on and come back inside. But if they're happy to see GD Dog then the owners are probably cool and will give us all the information we need plus some. And I promised GD Dog he could come. Let's go find out."

Going inside GD Dog was treated like royalty. The receptionist/office manager, who introduced herself as Judy, was a dog lover and after asking if it was okay to pet him did so behind the ears. What JR liked about her is that she didn't make fun of GD Dog. She even had a couple of dog treats in her desk and after asking if GD Dog could have one, and JR saying "Yes, but say, "Sam's old as dirt" and watch what he does."

Judy did as JR instructed.

GD Dog sat down, smiled and sat up on his back folded legs. Giving GD Dog the treat she looked at JR and Maggie and said that made her day with a smile from ear to ear.

Definitely a dog lover.

 Walking JR and Maggie back to an office Maggie was thinking and amazed that GD Dog had any talents. Things were not always what they appeared.

Meeting the owner who they were told to call Jim, and having Judy tell Jim how smart GD Dog was they took a seat across from a large desk. And a large desk was necessary for Jim whom Maggie was betting was called Big Jim, due to his size.

Starting off, Jim told Maggie and JR that he gave everyone from the police to OSHA everything he had from documentation of the ladder to the shoes they required roofers to wear.

"They went through this business with a fine tooth comb. Especially OSHA. After the fines from OSHA for not wearing a harness or having a spotter or this and that not being done to code, we almost lost the business. Especially when we had Ryan's wife's lawyer wanting to sue us for not having the proper training. Shit, Ryan was the trainer. He taught half the guys that are working here,"

"Julie sued your company?" Maggie wanted to make sure she heard that right.

"Yes. Everything is sealed and I'm not allowed to discuss, but yes. That's all I'm allowed to say about that. But I can say that the woman is a bitch.

JR found that damn interesting but what he wanted to know about was Ryan and the ladder.

"Jim, did you personally look at the ladder?"

" Of course I did. From top to bottom. That was a good ladder, OSHA approved and even after the fall it was in tip top shape. No one wanted to use it so it went for scrap aluminum. "

JR could tell that if Jim said he inspected the ladder after the accident then finding the ladder wouldn't matter.

"Jim, just between us three here, what do you think happened?"

GD Dog barked. "Sorry, four of us here."

Maggie looked at GD Dog and she swore he smiled at her.

"Everyday this accident plays out in my mind. And I've run through every scenario and I'm telling you that I hired Ryan when we were both young and the one thing I know is he would never let a ladder tip over because of footing. Never. And I think you two know I'm right and that's why you're here. I know about the last husband and his "accident". Hell everyone around here does. She's getting away with another one. I don't know how but the bitch is smiling all the way to the bank.``

Maggie had to ask, "We understand Ryan might have had a drinking problem"

"First it wasnt "Might ". No, he had a drinking problem. But Ryan was a working alcoholic. I go home, have a few beers, relax and go back to work bright and early. Ryan couldn't have just a few beers. Once he started he just kept on going. That man could drink anyone underneath the table but he was used to it. What happened to Ryan was that Julie started partying with him the last few months before his accident. Or so he said and I believed him. But I'm telling you that Ryan could come in and outwork any one on any crew, and he would never, and let me say this again, never use a ladder that was not stabilized correctly."

Maggie asked Jim what happened to the tiles that were broken. Were they ever replaced? And who called it in?

Jim smiled. "That's another strange thing. As I'm sure you know we received a call from a person saying they were out in their yard on a ladder and noticed that this property had a few busted tiles next to the chimney and that they were concerned since they were calling for rain. They were going to call the home owners and let them know. They did not leave a name or a number, and as far as those damn tiles? Ryan did caulk them, and they were broken. At first I thought they were placed in there to close together and the house had some major expansion and retraction but these tiles looked like rocks had been dropped on them. But not a piece of rock or any debris anywhere."

"Could a pellet gun or a 22 rifle do it?" JR wanted to know.

"No. I know what that looks like. These tiles didn't just have one cental hole like a gun would make, these tiles were cracked in several small places. It looked like somehow a bunch of good sized rocks were thrown up on the roof, but nothing. Not even in the gutters. I even thought of a shotgun loaded with salt pellets but this breakage was concentrated in just one area."

JR didn't want to hear that.

Maggie and JR asked a few more not so important questions and told Jim he had been more than helpful. JR asked Jim if he would like to come over at eleven thirty the following day to see the ladder set up and stay for lunch. Bring Judy along if she would like to come along. Big Jim. said he would definitely be there and most likely Judy.

Heading back to home base with GD Dig sitting on her lap Maggie was happy. Those people were nice. The meeting went well and she was going to be seeing her love of her life soon.

Something occurred to Maggie out of the blue. Looking at JR she said, "Ice?"

JR looked at Maggie and smiled. "Maybe."

Maggie asked how the ice got up there. Saying she didn't think could stand on the ground and keep throwing big chunks of ice till those certain tiles broke.

"I'm not sure but I'm leaning towards a ladder. And before you ask, take a minute and google "Telescoping 30 foot ladder."

Doing so Maggie was impressed with today's technology.

"Shit they got one that fits in the trunk of a car. Here I'm picturing someone toting around this huge ladder."

"And did you look at weight? Under 80 lbs. One physically fit lady could handle that with ease."

"Maggie even if we figure out how they broke the tiles or how they moved the ladder it isn't going to do shit. What we do know is that they had to practice somewhere and they had to purchase these items and not leave a trace anywhere. What's that tell you?"

The two never spoke another word till they were almost home.

Turning and looking at JR, Maggie said, "I got it."

"Took you long enough."

Smiling Maggie said, "Fuck you JR."

Chapter 11

Pulling into the driveway at JR's house Maggie saw her Doc unloading groceries from his car.

JR smiling said to Maggie that he knew what she would be doing for the next couple of hours.

"As I said, Fuck You JR. I don't cook. If god had wanted us to cook he wouldn't have made restaurants or delivery. Or microwaves. Or fast food."

Helping the Doc in with the groceries JR was surprised to hear nothing. The house was quiet. Looking outside he saw no one by the pool. GD Dog turned and looked at JR.

"Hey Doc, where the hell is everyone?"

"Well when you and Maggie left everyone was just sitting there discussing what they were going to do until Rita said she was going on the computer to figure out where the practice property was. She suggested that the guys go to Home Depot and start recreating the accident scene down to the last block. She told the ladies nicely that she could use some help on the computers. So I'm betting the ladies are still in the computer room."

Laughing JR asked how Sam took it.

"You know Sam. He bitched and complained but it was more for show. I have a feeling that he was probably going to do it anyway. I thought I'd go with the guys but Rita stopped me and told me I had a dinner to cook and a woman to impress.

Walking back to the computer room with Maggie in tow after she told the Doc she'd be back in a minute, they were both surprised as they got closer to hear Michelle's voice speaking in Spanish. Maggie was more surprised then JR since he at least knew Michelle was fluent in the language along with four others.

The ladies were smiling and brought their fingers up to their lips in a shushing gesture.

Waiting a couple more minutes Michelle hung up the phone and looking at JR said "We got it."

JR knew it had to be good because all the ladies' faces lit up in huge smiles.

"The property?"

"No, the divorce papers.. Of course the property!"

Tina who was back on the computer asked JR to come take a look at a picture she had pulled up on her computer.

As she zoomed in JR turned and looked at Rita and said "Holy shit. Ladies, you are the best. Have you seen this?"

Rita came over and looked at the picture and then looked at JR. "What now, JR?"

Finding the property brought with it a whole new set of problems.

" Whose name is it in?" JR asked

Tina answered. "Maria Gonzales."

Rita gave JR the short version on how it came to be.

Taking a minute to collect his thoughts he knew what needed to be done.

"Ladies, this work is fantastic, but for now we are going to have to be very cautious and make sure this isn't another set up. Tina, can you use that address and find out about the cable, internet, electricity, garbage pick-up and phone? Rita can you get ahold of one of the three stooges and tell them not to unload anything out of the van? Leave everything in the van. We want no sign that they were at home depot. Next we need our lawyer and Phil on speaker phone in the dining room asap. Michelle I need you to tell Phil and our lawyer exactly what transpired and the conversion you had on the phone . I'm going to assume that Tim and Laurie are out taking a casual walk looking for cameras. Katie, please get a hold of one of them and tell them their needed in here asap."

As JR was contemplating their next move Tina said to JR that that address has a phone, internet and all the premium channels plus NetFlix.

"Whose name is it in?"

"Maria Gonzoles."

JR looked at Michelle who just shook her head yes and smiled. JR couldn't wait to hear the whole story.

Rita had called Sam and gave him the instructions. She looked at JR and asked what the problem was.

"We can't touch that house until we find out legally who owns it. I didn't even have to ask cause I know it's not in Julies or any of that crazy family's name. We step one foot on that property and we might be trespassing. Maybe. Let's get the lawyers to figure this out and do it by the book. These bitches always seem to be one step in front of us. What we need is a little bit of luck, And like I said, we're doing this legally.

"That will be a change," someone said. JR thought it was Tina. She really was acting more like Sam everyday

While Laurie was setting up the conference call, Tim told JR that he could verify only one remote camera in a palm tree in an adjacent neighbor's house quite aways down the road. It wouldn't give them great visibility but they could probably make out the driveway and give them a good idea who was here.

JR smiled and thanked both of them.

Setting up the speaker phone, everyone got comfy to hear Michelles tale.

"Phil, I wanted you and Greg to hear what the ladies found out regarding a piece of property we had been looking for and afterward tell us who owns it."

Greg was the S and W lawyer who the State of Florida had tried to disbar more than once. This man was one the smartest men JR knew when it came to Florida Law and wouldn't trust him with his wallet but he was shrewd, intelligent and knew Florida Law better then just about anyone.

Michelle began. "Hey guys, I'm going to start at the beginning and give you the short version. We have four suspects we are looking at past and present at a property the suspects we believe had access to in the past years. We found that one of the suspects was in the military and stationed at MacDill Air Force Base. While there she rented an apartment off base with another woman who was in the military. By chance we ran her name and found that she owned an acre of land in Homosassa out in the boonies. Her name was Maria Gonzales. Then by chance Rita ran a search on this lady and she came up as deceased. After some more searching we found her grandmother who lived in Peru. Calling her she said she knew about the property which her granddaughter and her friend had said was out in the country somewhere in Florida that had a small trailer on it. And she even met our suspect twice. The first time was when they took leave and came to visit her. They had explained that they had bought the property together and were using it as an investment for when the two got out of the service. It wasn't that much longer after their visit she got a visit from a military chaplain and another person saying her granddaughter had died in a drowning accident in Puerto Rico while on leave. Her granddaughter had left her military life insurance policy to her which she thought was a very nice thing to do. A couple of days later our suspect showed up and after giving her condolences asked if she would have any problem if she kept the property. She would give the grandmother the money that her granddaughter had invested in it which was $3,000.00. The grandmother had almost forgotten about the property and was more than happy to receive the extra money. Plus, seeing how bereaved our suspect was, she agreed and signed a piece of paper that our suspect said was just a basic ownership form. I asked how long this form was and she told me a couple of pages. That was the last she heard from our suspect. What we did find out is that the property is and has always been in Maria's name. Our suspect's name appears nowhere.. That's the short version.

JR was so glad that Michelle gave them the short version. Tina passed JR the laptop "Guys, Tina checked and the cable and phone are still in the granddaughter's name."

Tina who had been on her laptop the entire time said they could also include electricity and the taxes are up to date also in the granddaughter's name.

Peter, who had remained silent, asked, "So basically this property is owned by a dead person while someone is paying the bills in her name?"

Yes

"And I'm betting you want a search warrant?"

"Yes. And to take the computer and some additional hardware."

"All right, bear with me for a minute and Phil you tell me what you think. As of now you folks there at S and W are the only ones who know who's using that trailer and paying the bills which I'm betting are going to the trailer. Now if you went inside the trailer and video taped everything and took a few things who would press charges? I'm betting the suspect had granny sign a form stating that she was selling the trailer to your suspect. I'm saying that because the granddaughter most likely left everything to her since she got the life insurance policy. So legally as of now your suspect does own the trailer Your suspect never had it transferred and she's technically been forging checks for awhile. Michelle, what was granny's full name?"

"Her name is Theresa Maria Gonzolas."

"And the granddaughters name whose name is on all the paperwork?"

"Maria Gonzolas."

Peter chuckled and told everyone that today was S and W's lucky day.

"That makes it a lot easier. Everything is still in Maria Gonzoles name. So as far as the court and government knows it belongs to granny. Phil, do you agree with me?"

He did.

"So this next part is going to cost you some money. What you have to do is talk to granny, tell her the property that she signed over to your suspect is being used for illicit purposes and their using her granddaughters name for ill purposes. What you want to do is have granny sign paperwork selling you the property. You're going to need the paperwork in hand for the police if they are called by your suspects. Is Sam there?"

Sam and the guys had come in a few minutes ago and were told to not say a word by the Doc before he could make a ruckus. Standing there he said he was but "he didn't know shit about what was going on."

Rita told him she'd explain everything but for now just listen.

"Sam, your friend the Lieutenant needs to help out. After Rita explains everything you'll see what you need. Make sure the police in Homosassa understand and that S and W has permission to be there legally. You'll figure it out. Next , Phil, you get that paperwork written up and fast and get it down there to Peru to one of your homies. You email or fax it asap. And get some money down there so they can pay the local police, you know how it works. And now you, JR, get some people headed up to Homasasa with a portable fax machine and laptop and printer. As soon as you get that paperwork you're all set. And I plan on billing S and W for two hours work. Phil, you let me know if you need anything. Now I'm off to rip another unsuspecting customer. You folks take care."

JR told Peter not so fast.

"What you don't know is that there are four suspects that are smart and one of them is Michelle smart and one knows computers and hardware. Three sisters and a mother. And they're smart. Very, very smart. And no, we are not running up to Homasasa and taking control until later. Peter you can bet your ass they have already talked to a lawyer and may have planned for this and as soon as we pull into that property there's a good chance they may know. We need you to verify that this will be legal. Contact anyone you need to. Pay them cash for their time but check and then double check everything then call Phil. And could you please write up what you would consider the proper documentation for granny to sign. Then send it to Phil."

"Are they that smart?"

"Yes "

Peter said he was on it. He didn't joke this time about charging S and W for his time.

Phil said he had to run but before he could hang up Tina asked him to stay on for a few more minutes.

Looking at JR she asked if he gave any thought besides walking in there and grabbing the computer and hardware and then just walking out?

JR hadn't had time

"We won't bet on it. Phil while your talking to your Homeys, as Peter said , were going to need a bomb squad technician and their going have to be really, really good. Someone who has lots of experience. And they're going to need to be here in the next few hours if you plan on doing this tonight, which in reality I would do before one of the ladies gets edgy and drives there. They're almost done with the trailer and as soon as they are, you're going to have an explosion destroying everything."

JR was amazed. This is the most he had heard Tina speak at a meeting since she came on board.

"All right Phil, get us a bomb tech. And have your lovely wife call and wake up our Pilot and make sure the jet's fueled up and ready to fly anywhere and bring them to St. Petersburg or Tampa airport. Someone from S and W will pick them up and drive directly to the property.

Michelle spoke up and said she volunteered.

"NO!" It was said in unison by everyone.

"Phil I know you have plenty to do so real quick, who do we have available for a night time excursion that can drive one of the office vans that can bring it over here for dinner? Then drive to Homassa?

After telling JR that everyone was out on cases he said he'd have Barbara, his wife bring it over.

JR explained that whoever drove the van would be leaving and going to Homosassa with a van full of detectives in the back.

"And? She knows that's why we make the big money. She'll be there and know where she's going and be happier than hell. Alright I gotta go. Oh wait, what time is dinner? "

Laughing, JR told Phil to tell his wife to be here at six thirty.

 "Well that went better than expected. Before we go any further I say we take 15 minutes and go to the bathroom, get something to drink and stretch our legs. And Tina, Thank You. You did good. Really good. "

Everyone there agreed and said so.

Tina of course acted like it meant nothing but everyone knew she was proud.

Sam just said that he was teaching her well.

With that said, Tina actually smiled.

Fifteen minutes later everyone was in the dining room seated or standing as JR came back from taking GD Dog for a walk. JR had asked Michelle to go also but she said she had to use the bathroom and for those two to go ahead without her. Asking if she was okay she said she had eaten too many cucumbers in a salad and she thinks it messed with her stomach.

Giving her a hug and a kiss, saying he loved her he took a relaxing walk and thought about tonight and what needed to be done.

Back 15 minutes later he asked her if she was better. "Oh much. I just needed a good poop."

The meeting was quick and to the point. JR looking at everyone told them that Tina was right. They all had been underestimating these ladies till they almost got screwed. Tonight they were planning on the worst and hoping for the best. They were not going to underestimate them again.

"First , the good news. Laurie, you and Tim get to spend the night working together. I need you to figure out the outside lighting and camera system. Looking at the picture Tina has printed I would think the worst. We need to know what we're dealing with on the outside before we go inside."

Michelle had a glow about her as she interrupted JR. "Honey we have time, let's let Laurie and Tim tell us what they think we're dealing with first then you tell us what we're doing."

JR was happy, his wife was back.

Asking Tim about the outside cameras and how they could be disconnected he looked at his wife Laurie and said that most likely all cameras were run to a location on the right side box, just above where the ladder was sitting under a tarp. . It was probably locked with a hardened padlock which also could be booby trapped or to send a signal when opened. Of course this whole time they would be on camera until it was disconnected. So ......

"JR, you're not going to do it and I'm not losing you or any of my friends. Now take another look, I'll be right back."

Thirty seconds later Michelle came back carrying an easel with a pad of drawing paper on it. Drawing a rectangular square in the middle she asked Laurie to point out where they thought the cameras were.

Between her and Tim they gave an estimate of where they thought the cameras would be located and the motion detection cameras.

"Babe, this helps but we have to be exact."

Not saying a word she looked ar GD Dog. Everyone there then looked at GD Dog. He wasn't smiling. Actually he gave a little growl.

"SO now you know with GD Dog's help where all the motion activated lighting is and I'd bet the camera system is tied in with them. Lights come on, camera starts rolling. You two agree?"

They did.

"Okay, let's assume, since that's all we can do for now, that that's it for the cameras. Laurie you and Tim draw on here what range and area the cameras would be covering. I know it's just a guess but give it your best."

The two discussed what size lighting and make of camera that they could have possibly used and taking the marker drew in circles where they thought the area would be illuminated and observed by the remote cameras,

Tim told the group that without actually seeing what lighting and cameras and how they were positioned this would have to do.

Sam wanted to know if there was a chance they used stronger lighting.

"Of course they could have but they don't want to draw attention to the place either. They just want regular lighting like their neighbors down the road probably have. And we're going with the assumption they used six cameras which in reality I'm betting they just used four , one on each corner. We're figuring six to give you the max we believe they could use. They did not want the house lit up like the fourth of July every time an animal walked through that area. Hell, squirrels alone could activate the system for a couple of hours. This lighting is used more than anything as a deterrent. I'm betting they don't even check it when it's activated till the next day, if then. If it was us, your main alarm is tied into the doors and windows."

Michelle asked, "What about the roof?"

No one said a word.

"I mean look, we're going to spend hours trying to figure out this alarm system and chances are we still won't be 100 percent positive." Michelle walked over to the easel and said, "What would happen if you cut a roofing panel, say over top of the incoming utility box, remove the insulation panel, cut the next panel and presto your in."

Everyone looked at JR.

"Tina, can we print out a close up of the roof?"

Tina was back in 2 minutes with two pictures in hand. Telling JR that she couldn't fit the entire roof in one picture he would need to put them together.

Putting them together he smiled.

JR passed the pictures around. "Looks like we have our way in."

What everyone saw when they looked at the picture was an old, dirty, debris covered tin roof.

Sam seeing the pictures said a can opener could open this roof.

JR looked at everyone and said. "The roof it is."

JR told everyone that Sam, Tim or Laurie, Thomas and David would be going along with JR and the Demo person. Barbara of course was driving. Right now he needed the ladies to go outside. He wanted whoever was watching them to think the men were waiting inside to hear how the detective involved in the accident was doing. The guys were going to get everything ready to be loaded into Barbara's van.

" When Barbara is almost here, Rita, you and Katie will be going to pick up beer or whatever in one of the vans parked in the garage. You'll leave the garage door open . Barbara is going to pull into the spot you just left. When Rita returns she's going to park behind any other van. Rita and Katie are going to take the beer and walk in through the garage shutting the garage door behind them. We'll come out and put everything in Barbara's van. Right before we say goodnight the folks going to Homosassa will be in the van and off we go.

The next 25 to 30 minutes had the guys loading everything by the door leading into the garage. Finished, the men went outside where Laurie asked Tim if he remembered this and that. It was getting close to six thirty and Rita and Katie asked if anyone needed anything.

The plan went according to plan. So far so good but the night was just beginning JR thought to himself.

It was almost 9 oclock and no one had heard from Phil. JR knew they couldn't wait much longer and that they may just have to go someplace and park when Phil called JR's cell.

"Hey buddy, just thinking of you."

"What a fucking night but I'm done. Your demo person will be waiting in Tampa in 1 hour. I'm emailing over everything to the vans computer. Your paperwork is on its way to and you should have it in about an hour also. It will also be sent over to the van. Peter said the place is yours once she signs. At least for now.. Now if you don't have any questions I'm going to go make a pitcher of very strong Margaritas and sit in the Jacuzzi. And I better not get any phone calls saying something happened to my wife.``

JR promised Phil she would be coming home in one piece.

All the guys and equipment were crammed in the back of the van . It ended up Tim going and was leaving Laurie to monitor everything remotely.

"I told Laurie that she could go but I was told she watched Sam eat two helpings of Doc's shrimp with rice and beans. I don't think we could have paid her extra to go."

JR looked at Sam. "Really?"

"What? I was hungry and I'd get ready cause I feel it brewing."

Sam wasn't lying. By the time they got to the waiting parking area at Tampa airport not one soul in the van could wait for it to stop and depart (run like hell) from inside the van. It looked like a chinese fire drill.

Poor GD Dogs eyes were watering and looked at JR as if to say "Make it stop".

Chapter 11

The demo expert was supposed to call Barbara when she was out in the pick-up zone. After picking her up and placing her equipment in the back which JR would grab, they pulled back around to the same waiting zone area. After introductions she would get in the back with the guys where JR would explain what was needed.. And Sam would ride up front.

Once again everything went as planned. Driving back around to the waiting area and parking in the back the guys did the same exiting as before.

JR, Seeing the captain for the first time, his first thought was this was a captain in the military. She stood tall, rigid and had that air about her as always being on guard, looking for anything that could mean danger. With graying blond hair and wire framed glasses he guessed she was nearing fifty or close.

Introducing himself and the rest of the guys she saw GD Dog.

The captain looked at JR and said "Thats the ugliest Fucking Dog I have ever seen." Bending over she picked GD Dog up and said. "Hey your a boy dog. I bet you're smarter than shit." She petted and held GD dog as they talked.

JR liked her already. So did GD Dog. He wasn't thrilled about the ugliest dog comment. Sam, of course being Sam, checked her fingers and asked if she had all her toes.

"All here and you smell like beer. So be a gentleman and offer a lady one. That's got to be the worst pilot and flight I have ever been on. And trust me, I flew with a one armed pilot once."

Sam liked her already.

JR explained that he'd like the captain to ride in the back so he could explain tonight's excursion while Sam rode in the front to allow them to breathe. The captain didn't say a word, just got in and asked where to sit. Giving her the office chair in front of the computer, JR knelt next to her and explained the scenario from start to finish.

 The captain just listened, never asking a question until the end,

 "Are they that smart?" was all she asked.

 JR was honest. "Whatever you're thinking, times it by ten. These bitches are smart and whatever you assume, please think the worst. "

 Just before turning off the major freeway to take the small double lane road to Homosassa, Barbara pulled into the last rest area before they had to turn off. Barbara, who had to deal with Sam and his gas and his jokes came up to JR and politely told him that he was driving home and he could deal with Sam. Sam of course was laughing.

 JR had given everyone a few minutes to stretch their legs and use the bathroom before he handed a couple of pictures around of the overall view of the property surrounding the area. JR explained his plan as Captain Neal stood close listening.

 The first part of the plan was relatively simple. JR would cut through the vegetation on the back side of the house where the vegetation seemed to be the lightest. Then he'd get in position and Sam would let GD Dog loose to go running to JR activating the cameras and lighting. After a couple of minutes JR would move to the front of the property letting GD Dog loose where he would go running to Sam, again activating ihe cameras and lighting."

 JR explained that If anyone was watching the camera system chances are that the person watching would just assume it was a dog again and pay no intention.

 Sam would have the ladder ready to go and set it up after a location was decided on where to cut through the roof. JR would go first followed by Tim would hold the flashlight as JR cut through. Once the roof was opened Tim would drop down followed by the Captain and JR. The Captain and Tim would access what was involved and if possible deactivate everything but to not take any chances they would just bring the computer and phone recording machine back through the hole JR had cut. They would load up and adios.

 The captain who had not said a word finally spoke. "Guys, would you mind if I make a few suggestions? Before I do, let me explain that at one time I held the rank of a Major in the Military. I was one of the lead officers in charge of the demolition instructors. Chances are if they were in the military anything they know one of my instructors who I trained, trained them. If you would allow me I would like to run this operation with you and save some lives or at least get you home in one piece. Now JR your plan is sound. And we are going with it but with a few modifications. "

 JR knew that she was speaking the truth and said so. "Captain, we're all equal here and any help you can give is greatly appreciated."

"All right. First thing first. I need another beer then I'm going to pee and then the games will begin."

She asked JR what time it was.

"Almost 10:30"

"We're not going to start until eleven so let's run down to that convenience store we passed and grab some more beer and water and grab some Pepto Bismol for Sam. When we get back I'll be going underneath the trailer for a sweep and then drill some holes if it's safe and insert a camera up so we can see what we're dealing with before any boots hit that floor."

That thought had never occurred to anyone listening.

The Captain knew how everyone was feeling. "Guys, I've been doing this for over thirty years. Your plan is sound. It most likely would have worked with or without me. All I'm doing is giving you a few extra odds in your favor.

Sam whispered to JR as they headed to the Van, "Can we keep her?"

"Let's see how the night goes first." JR liked having better odds. He just prayed she was up to it.

As the guys put on their camouflage jump suits and strapped their earpieces on the Captain looked at them all and asking in a statement, "You fucking guys are ex-milirary?"

"At S and W sometimes nothing seems like it appears."

Handing her a headset he explained that she would be able to communicate with all the detectives including the ones at home base. She also received a head mounted camera that would allow everyone to see what she saw.

JR explained that there were five of the smartest women and one slightly demented doctor who couldn't play poker worth shit at home base that would be watching on the computer screens everything she saw. Also the telescoping cameras she would be inserting into the holes she would be drilled were wireless so the scanner would give them a direct feed.

JR highly recommended she give them a slow sweep and wait till they said it was okay to move on to the next room.

"Next room? I'm not sure where the first hole I'm going to drill will end up."

Michelle's voice came over the headsets, "Don't worry captain, we will give you an estimate as soon as you give us a picture underneath. We'll walk you through it."

"Who is this?

"It's Michelle and it's nice to say hello. Everyone here really appreciates your help and says "Hi". And you keep our husband safe and we're also having a luncheon tomorrow and of course you're invited. And don't worry, you're spending the night at our house. And I hope you brought a bathing suit because......."

Rita spoke and reminded Michelle they were working.

"Sorry, Can't wait to meet you Captain."

The Captain looked at JR and said, "Bathing Suit?"

JR smiled and told the Captain what was even scarier was that was his wife.

The plan of GD Dog doing his routine went perfectly. Lighting went on, little red lights on the cameras clicked on and the group decided that the least amount was on the back of the house facing the woods. The lighting there was weak and if someone knew how to deactivate the window alarm they could almost go right in.

Sam looked at JR and told him it almost looked too easy.

The Captain smiled and agreed.

It was decided then that the front right corner would then be the spot. The Captain and Thomas went low to the block skirting and removed a section of block that was large enough for the captain to slip through. Once in, JR ran up and threw a duffel bag through. JR and Thomas then hastily replaced the block and running low went to the van where everyone was watching the video feed from the Captains camera.

They could hear Michelle telling the Captain they needed two scans and to point the camera up to the top and do a slow scan of the trailer's flooring and then do a slow scan of the bottom.

Showing the bottom of the flooring above was actually easy. All the original insulation was now laying on the ground. No one had invested any money on maintaining any upkeep on this place for years. It did make it easy to spot any wiring or devices that could create an obstacle as far as security systems. The only thing visible was the plumbing and the old cable television cables that were originally run when cable TV was first introduced to this remote area.

Once that was completed Michelle said it was okay to drill a hole and if she counted 4 floor joists out and an arms length out from the front wall she would be fine.

The captain drilled a ½" inch hole and inserted the camera. Everyone watched as a single bed came into view. Scanning the room the walls showed no decorations or pictures. The only furniture beside the bed was an older three drawer dresser that had a newer 32" television setting on top.

A voice she had never heard before told the Captain to point the camera slowly to the window facing the front then to the window facing the side one more time,

Seeing the wiring attached to each window and running on top of the interior walls, the Captain was getting ready to say they were probably run in a series but had a feeling to keep her mouth shut,

Another lady the captain had heard just once, telling Michelle they had to work, told the Captain to head slowly to the next room. Crawling about ten feet the lady came back on and told the Captain that she was approaching the front door and to go even slower.

Michelle said stop.

"Captain, slowly point your camera 3 feet in front and above you."

Doing so the Captain saw a coaxial cable that looked like it had been underneath for years.

"All right, Captain, you're in the living room. That's a coaxial cable in front of you which probably is just an old tv cable but let's avoid it. What I need you to do right now is to your right is a metal duct running from the back of the trailer to the front. Slowly make your way to that duct."

Once the Captain reached the trunk line the lady Michelle said to go ahead and drill a hole 6 inches from the trunk line facing the entry wall. Doing so and inserting and pointing the camera towards the front, the Captain saw the front door along with 2 windows next to it, a computer, printer and a telephone answering machine sitting on two end tables with a piece of plywood acting as a desk. In the opposite direction, on the right hand exterior wall were 2 windows with an old couch facing the front wall. An older 27" television was mounted on the middle wall exactly where the cable came up. Pointing the camera into the section she was heading she saw a very small kitchen with a two seat cheap dinette table and chairs.

  The camera had just missed the couch.. The only furniture besides the couch was an old wooden end table with a newer lamp with no shade on it.

  Telling the Captain to do a very slow scan top to bottom the ladies and the Captain on her small screen could find nothing. The windows had the same security

  JR kept silent and let the Captain continue along with the ladies' help. What surprised everyone but JR was back in the far corner that they had expected to find trip wires or some other kind of device but there was nothing ,, nada. Only the windows and front door showed any wiring. The Captain slowly crawled down the back side of the mobile home until Michelle said to stop and drill a hole and insert the camera. Activated the camera showed a set of six heavy duty batteries sitting on a steel shelving unit. On the side wall was a small gasoline powered generator. Between the shelving and the batteries was a medium size electrical panel box with 2 metal utility boxes mounted adjacent to the electrical panel boxes. On the far rear wall JR could make out the older original panel box and a small closet with two sliding doors. On the interior wall next to the door sat a cheap beat up end table bearing an internet modem box which had one Cat-5 internet line plugged in which was running to the ceiling. JR was betting that if you followed it around it would lead to the computer in the living room. Also was one phone line that he was betting that when they followed it around, they ran through to the telephone and answering machine which was sitting next to the computer.

  Speaking into his head set JR told the Captain she was just about done underneath. Asking Michelle and the ladies to guide the Captain to the bathroom and complete a slow span and once that was completed to do one more. This time in front of the front door. The last request JR had was for Tina to send over the mobile home blueprint of the mobile home. And a picture of the bathroom.

  No one asked JR what was going on. Sam, for one of the few times, kept quiet.

  Watching as the video of the bathroom was shown, JR grabbed the blueprint of the mobile home, a beer and went and sat on the ground next to GD Dog who was watching the coming and goings waiting next to Sam.

  Asking Sam to hold a flashlight, JR finished looking at the pages and thought to himself how smart those ladies were. Thinking about it a smile came across his face. Telling Sam thanks for holding the light JR finished his beer and waited till the Captain had a fresh beer before asking, "We'll folks how hard is it to get in the front door? Captain?"

After taking a large gulp of beer, The Captain looked at JR and said, "This may have been the easiest money I ever made. A high school kid could have put in this security system by reading the installation instructions off a kit off Amazon."

JR smiled. " I agree with you as I'm sure everyone who saw the video does also. There is just one big problem we overlooked."

 JR knew this was too easy. These ladies had used this computer for everything and just left it out there for anyone to grab. He didn't think so..

"We're assuming again. Listen, those ladies can't call the police and do not want the police here. They're not going to call the police if their computer is stolen or if anything is stolen for that matter. No, that computer is a security system computer. We see the lines running in the back where all the security lines are tied in and that's real but that's all that's on there. What we're probably going to find is that in each duct or somewhere in each room is a wireless speaker just loud enough for the people inside to hear or it could be a siren or a vicious dog. It could be someone talking saying get the hell out of here or a number of things. The lighting inside is all probably going to be motion activated if someone makes it past the dogs barking or whatever they used then the lightings going to scare the hell out of whoever's trying to come in.

 I'm not saying there's not going to be maybe a few more surprises but I'm telling you that's not the computer we want. And one last thought, say a couple young stupid kids break in. There half baked and say fuck it, were going inside.

 They rip the wiring and steal the computer. Getting it home someone decides to open it and it explodes and takes out a finger or two or an eye. The cops would be called and Little Joey, his partner in crime, says where they got it.. Noo, I'm thinking these ladies want to keep everything hush hush. When this case settles down and one of them can make it out here safely then chances are everything in it will be burnt to the ground along with the computer that has everything on it that we're going to go get right now. And Captain, you're wrong. You and everyone here or listening are going to earn their money tonight. And we have to hurry cause right now having this place is the last evidence they know that could burn them. Or they could be thinking no one will ever find this place. Let's just keep it. But trust me this place along with the computer will be gone very soon. What's helping us right now is that they think no one knows or can find out about this place. And, we need to be back by six tomorrow morning and once they see that we're all there and setting up for the ladder scenario one or two of them may be coming to burn this place to the ground or some other way to get rid of the evidence. I'm betting on fire. This place is filled with their fingerprints, hair fibers and lord knows what else.``

Someone asked why they didn't just wear gloves and a hair net?

JR explained, "I thought the same thing. And they probably did at the beginning. But remember Kristen has the paperwork saying granny sold it to her. After a while they realized that no one was coming so guess what? This is now their vacation home and home base. And I have to respect these ladies. We never would have known about it if it wasn't for pure luck. And we don't realize how much dumb luck was involved. If we just had one person researching these ladies and they happened to research Kristen back to her military days, which is a long shot, and they saw she rented a place with Maria Gonzales and ran Maria's name they are going to pull up that she's deceased and move onto something else.

It was just by chance that Rita put Maria's name in the database before Tina or one of the other ladies found out she was deceased or it could have ended right there. Now these ladies are smart but one of the dumbest things those crazy bitches did was have Kristen go to Granny's house in Peru on leave with Maria. Maybe they didn't think Granny was going to live that long, Who knows. All I know is we now have them if we can get that computer out of this trailer. And I'll say one more interesting fact which was staring us in the face before we send the Captain back in. The emergency generator. We all saw those six heavy duty back up batteries and the generator. At first I was thinking it was for the security cameras and the security system but why the generator? Those six batteries should last for a long with just running a few amps off them. It would supply power for a few days. Now Tina, let me ask you a question. Say we put a computer in a hardened steel airtight container out in a tin box?"

"The computer and everything else in there would eventually start melting and the computer would have to have air for the fans. But JR you see the videos. We're seeing nothing there."

"It's there. We don't see it but it's there. It's a brain teaser for another day. Right now our goal is the computer and phone machine."

"What I would also bet money on is out in that shed. I'm betting we will find a couple of lounge chairs, maybe an old grill and a weed eater. They knew that as long as they kept the weeds down to a minimum, made the place appear as if people were using it on the weekends or as a place for a family on vacation they could do what they wanted. The part that got me is when Tina said they have Netflix. If you're coming in to just use the computer you don't order Netflix. Trust me, these bitches were using this place as home base."

Sam who had been listening while petting GD Dog told JR he would bet that there was a porta potty and a portable solar bag shower in there too. Everyone listening thought Sam was joking at first.

"Think about it. Say they burn down this place which will include the shed I'm sure. What's not going to burn? The damn septic system you morons."

Sam was right as usual.

JR explained at this time he was going to cut a hole in the front bedroom floor with Mark's help. The Captain would be standing by with her bomb suit which she will put on once she was through the hole.

"The Captain will then make her way to the bathroom and slowly do a pan of the cabinet next to the tub that has the water heater in.. Then she will go to the closet in the master bedroom that shares the same wall with the tub/ shower unit. If it hasn't been fucked with there shoud be an access panel which she will then remove."

JR told the Captain to be prepared for the unexpected. "They're going to scare you off before you get to the prize."

Rita told JR to slow down and please explain what's going on.

"Rita if I'm right then what we see is a medium grade security system on the front door and windows. Would you agree with that Tim? Laurie? Captain?"

All saying "yes" JR continued.

" Now I'm betting we could have walked right in here and taken that computer and phone machine and walked out and the police would never have been called. Busted door to get in? They would have fixed it along with a window themselves if the thieves had used it to break in. Think about it. NO POLICE. Police ask questions, first being who owns this place. So they put in a few deterrents like outside motion activated lighting, and I'm betting as I said a bunch of cheap motion activated lighting inside. And wireless speakers with something that is another deterrent. The prize computer is there and I'm betting it's in the bathroom. They removed the water heater and used that space. We keep overlooking what is right in front of us. How are the ladies communicating with each other? How did they research S and W? Theres a fucking computer and some sort of phone recording devise in that trailer and Tina was right. We need Captain Neal. These biches are even smarter than we thought."

Everything was going exactly as JR had said it would. Mafk and he had cut the hole in the floor and allowed the Captain to enter. Putting on her suit she proceeded slowly into the living room and could find no hidden traps so far. As the Captain slowly made her way into the bathroom she was pointing the camera down one of the AC vents and they could just make out a six inch wireless speaker. Passing a light switch they watched as an overhead fan with a ceiling light attachment came to life. The bulbs were brighter than the standard bulbs and let the room up like a Doctor's operating room. The Captain said that that does make it easier.

Making her way to the bathroom she raised her palm up and down in front of the light switch.Realizing that wasn't working she said, "NOO, of course not. Shit."

Moving her head head light around and turning on a very powerful flashlight she did a sweep of the room before heading to the sink base cabinet. Drilling the hole and inserting the camera the lady who was named Michelle, or as the Captain thought of her, crazy bitch, told her to stop and slowly remove her camera she had just inserted..

"Ahhh Michele what's going on?"

"It appears as if when you open the door something goes off. Wait,:

" Laurie said its a smoke bomb tied into a flash bomb. You can barely see the trip wire. Laurie says they use them to scare people or to use for cover."

"That sure the hell would have done it. I definitely would have had to change my panties. Thank you. Let's pass on this cabinet, for now. I'm off to the master bedroom closet now.

Again no hidden trip wires or tricks could be found. Before opening the sliding closet doors the Captain did a sweep of the door tracks and proceeded to drill a small hole in the one that was closest to the interior wall. Michelle said hold on before telling her it was clear.

Sliding open the door the Captain was on her toes for anything but as the crazy lady had said, it was clear.

Using one of her insulated Phillips screwdrivers the captain very slowly removed the old shower access panel. Once she was sure there were no trip wires she pointed her light

inside and saw insulation which she cautiously moved aside. Her light reflected back at her
."

   "JR, are you seeing this?"

   "I do and I was expecting that. We will find the same on the outside and the other sides
of the wall. What I need you to do is go back to the bathroom and use your screwdriver
and remove the two screws holding the overflow drain cover to the tub. Then if we get
lucky the drain might slide down enough so a hole isn't necessary and we can slip the
camera in."

   They didn't get lucky.

   Tim had given the Captain a small cordless drill in the kit and some standard bits.

   Drilling a hole in the old drain pipe was slow going. After a couple of minutes of getting
nowhere JR said to stop and that he was coming in. Carrying a larger electric drill and an
extension cord JR handed the captain both and told her to plug it in once he was gone..
Shit, he just remembered.

   "Hold on for a minute". Saying over his mike for Mark to grab the coldest water they had
and bring it to the opening.

   "Captain, I'm not sure but I'm betting they have a high heat device located somewhere. I
can't believe they have a fire and let the metal container survive. With the water we need
you to every few seconds cool the bit down and use the water freely.``

   The captain had already thought of this and was getting ready to mention this when JR
had thought of that. Maybe these people werent so dumb.

   Mark brought 4 beers to the opening saying the beer was ice cold where the water was
still warm. He also said Sam was crying about using his beer instead of water.

   The Captain was just happy it wasn't her beer.

   Handing the Captain the beers JR explained that he was sure it wouldn't take all of the
cans.

   The drill was high speed with a carbon bit that could drill through hardened steel like
butter. With the older brass elbow she was drilling through it went through easily.

   Inserting the camera and bending it upwards the Captain was surprised to see a piece of
plastic explosives mounted underneath a piece two by three . Continuing sliding the
camera up the view was obstructed by a piece of metal which probably held the computer.

   JR saw the problem and told the Captain that he was bringing in a pipe wrench and
would grab a chair for her to stand on so she could remove the shower head and do the
same as the tub overflow drain.

   Removing the shower head took the Captain appling all her weight to get the shower
stem to move but in the end it broke free almost causing the chair to tip over.

   "JR, could you add a small step stool to your inventory?"

   Drilling the hole in the opening left by the shower stem went as easily as before.
Inserting the camera into the hole and pointing it downwards showed a whole new
perspective. Wires were shown neatly secured and it also showed the medicine cabinet
with wires attached along with wires running up and down and sideways.

JR was pleased that the Captain had got them this far. Asking if everyone had enough video to decipher the system set up and being informed they did, he told the Captain to get out of her suit and come on out and drink a cold one.

The Captain didn't argue.

Twenty Minutes later Michelle said they had it figured out. Almost.. JR hated the almost part.

"We have the wiring figured out with one wire that comes off the medicine cabinet switch.. It's a regular 2 wire switch with one wire going to one side of the medicine cabinet and the other wire going to a post on the wood frame. If you try to remove the cabinet you're going to break contact setting off the explosive. We know how to work the latches to get the cabinet out but we have no idea where these wires run too. They dont run up or down but sideways into the Master bedroom's interior wall."

JR asked to have a picture of both the bathroom wall and the bedroom wall sent over. Laurie took control of the vans computer and seeing the pictures said it would be no problem.

JR grabbed a utility knife and a crow bar and headed back to the trailer. He asked Tim if he would mind setting the captain up a Utility bag with plenty of jumpers and to stand by for anything else she may need.

Turning he looked at the Captain and asked if she was ready for one last trip?

Telling JR she would be ready in five minutes after she finished her beer and took a piss.

Sam really liked her.

Before leaving JR asked the detectives to think about what they were supposed to do once they had the computer and hardware safely away.

JR went in first and as the captain was putting on her bomb suit went into the Master bedroom and cut the panelling with the knife allowing an opening about three feet by four feet directly where a towel bar was located. By this time the Capatain had entered dressed in her bomb suit.

Handing her the crow bar JR again made a hasty retreat.

The paneling was so old and dry that it came off in almost one sheet. There were some splintered edges but JR had cut it more than wide and long enough. Removing the paneling exposed 2 sets of switches which everyone knew were to the back of the towel bar holders. There was a problem for everyone watching except one. Whoever had installed the switches has used a type of foam to cover the backs of the switches so no screws or terminals were exposed.

The captain just said, "Why can't anything be easy?"

Taking out a set of what appeared to be roach clips she picked the smallest set and checked that they were working properly.

Satisfied she told everyone she was going to have to splice into one line at a time then run a jumper.

"Hey Sam if this son of a bitch blows you can drink my beer."

"You didn't have to tell me that. I'm already eyeing it since you used most of my good beer to drill some stupid holes."

Laughing, the Captain removed her gloves and set the head set down so everyone could watch as she worked. They watched as she put on magnifying glasses and taking one wire at a time applied pressure slowly until the clips snapped. Once finished she placed a jumper wire from one clipper to the other. Finished she said, here comes the moment of truth and cut the wires going to the switches.

Putting her headset on said, "Easy Peasies. What's next?"

Told that she could remove the medicine cabinet now she listened as Michelle explained how to remove it . Removing some old vitamin bottles and some very old Geritol, the captain did as instructed.   The medicine cabinet was heavy. They had used reinforced steel plating to create the same seal as they had done on the other side. The Captain almost dropped it.

Once done Michelle continued. "Alright Captain. Here comes the fun part. If you look inside there is a micro switch hooked to the track that the shelf sets on. It runs to a contact switch that enables it. What we need you to do is roll out the shelf with your left hand slowly while keeping your camera pointed at the switch. We will tell you when to stop.

The Captain did as instructed and heard Michelle say 'Stop' when the shelf was 9 inches out .

"Okay Captain, you have two switches you're going to need to turn off. If you look to the rear and to the right you will see a toggle switch which you will need to turn off first. That will allow you to pull the shelf out further to reach the on/off push micro switch. And I know you're thinking how am I going to reach that toggle switch and it was Maggie who figured it out. You'll meet Maggie soon. She is a great person and we were hoping for her and the Doc......"

Rita cut her off.. " Michelle, we're on a time limit here, don't forget."

`` I'll tell you later. So anyways Maggie called JR on his cell and he's coming in right now to hand you a tool that should work. Just make sure you don't move the computer yet."

The Captain was thinking to herself it's going to be amazing if she makes it out of here alive. Betting her life on a crazy woman's instructions. It was then that JR appeared in the doorway handing the Captain a two foot wooden dowel with a wooden eye glued on the end. Leaving the Captain to admit the tool worked perfectly. Maybe the crazy lady wasn't so crazy. Flipping the switch off, Michelle told her she could go ahead and pull the computer out but just enough to turn the micro switch off and to pull the cover off the computer.

The Captain did as she was told as everyone watched.

A new voice that she had never heard came on.

"Captain, what we need for you to do is slowly remove the screws holding the cover on. It looks like there are only four so far. Remove the screws slowly until the cover appears loose. Then slowly lift the cover up and let's see what we have. We will all be watching here for trip wires."

Asking herself once again how she let herself get talked into this she did again as was instructed. The cover came off easily. Looking inside she saw a small charge of plastic explosives connected to a device she had never seen before.

The lady who had given the instructions came on and told her to hold for a minute. Coming back over the headset she told her that she was looking at a DS135 wireless transmitter that could be activated by a phone call followed by a series of numbers . Once activated it would send a small charge to the explosive which is why the batteries were inside with it.

"So all I have to do is cut the wires?" The Captain was amazed.

"Yes but you have to cut the positive first which appears to be the blue one but give us one more minute.

Coming back the lady said it was a go. Blue one.

Taking a small sharp pair of wire cutters from her bag she cut the wire. Nothing happened.

"Okay Captain. That's it. Tims coming in to take the computer and hook it up to a battery backup system. Nice working with you".

The captain had a gut feeling that they were missing something. "Michelle put a hold on that and give me a few minutes."

JR was getting ready to say the same thing.

Tina was looking at the wiring as was everyone at home base.

JR didn't hesitate. "Captain, don't touch anything. Leave everything just as it is. I'm coming in."

Going back inside the captain met JR at the bathroom door. The two discussed what else the crazy bitches could have done. They both knew that whatever was done had to have a switch that could manually be turned on and off. The Captain had the computer ready to go and all that was left was to pick it up and go. So what the hell were they missing? With the computer drawer now partially out it gave them access to the interior of the container which they never had before.

JR knew the best way to figure out a problem was to have everyone watch and talk it through.

"Sam, you see anything we could have missed? Anyone?"

Sam said he couldn't see anything. No one else said a word.

It was Mark who spoke up. "Tina, this is an older computer. How old you think it is?"

"Sweetie, by the looks it's probably at least 10 years old. Why?

"Because this looks like a hell of a lot of work to use the computer. Take out a medicine cabinet, turn off the towel switch and then a micro switch, then a regular switch and now we're adding another switch? And we're taking the phone recorder also, right?"

Tina answered yes.

"JR, do me a favor and check that phone line that plugs into the back of the answering machine and see if you can see where it comes out of that container and see if you can trace it back to the point of origin."

At that point JR knew what Mark was thinking and was happy he worked for S and W.

"Tina, do we really need the answering machine right now?"

"No, but I'm kind of lost here. There's no wire going to any plastic explosive and it appears clean."

JR asked Mark to explain it to everyone.

Mark, who was the strong silent type, was actually pretty at ease at talking to a group once he started talking.

"All right. Let's say JR right and one or two of these ladies came down at least once a week or every two weeks. Maybe more. Maybe less depending on their schedule. Now they could use the phone machine anytime. I'm sure they were using code words and what's nice about phone machines is you can dial in to check messages and change the greeting. Remember that case we did where they were using the computer but had code words on pet food advertisements? It's the same principle. And if you're coming down to stay or two or even three and you don't have to use the computer you're not going to go through all the rigamarole just to check the answering machine. I believe that the answering machine in there is just bullshit. Now something else we need to consider is that all we want is the modem. We don't want the screen or keypad or the mouse. The modems clean. You checked it and I think we need to check it again."

"Honey what the hell are we looking for?"

JR answered for Mark. "Tina, your man is a genius. It's a proximity switch. Nice work Mark! And you do have bragging rights over Sam for the next year. And ladies take your time. Let's make sure that when the Captain unplugs the keyboard, mouse and screen she can still come out and have a beer with Sam and the guys, and Barbara. We're leaving everything here except the modem. Is that okay with you Tina?"

It was.

"Okay Captain. We need you to take the cover off the computer one more time. You and the gang are going over it with a fine tooth comb. Take your time. When you're ready let us know and we will come up to the floor in the bedroom and take in from you. Any questions?"

Chapter 12

It was 20 minutes later that the ladies came on and said the Captain was making her way to the bedroom with the computer. They also said they found nothing and it was gone over inch by inch.

Sam came on the line and said they had to make another run to the convenience store since someone drank a few of the Captain's beer. He thought it was Barbara.

Loading up the Captain watched as two unmarked police cars pulled in. One officer wearing Lieutenant bars and another with Captain bars.

Sam saw that the one officer was carrying a 12 pack of a popular german beer along with a 12 pack of a popular american beer

"What the hell. You guys stop by the titty bar on the way here?"

"Fuck you Sam."

Putting the 12 packs close to Sam he was told that the refrigerator was inside .

Shaking his head he walked over to JR.

"We'll JR you certainly have had a busy night."

JR said he was glad it was over. "Did you see everything clearly?"

"Came in perfect. Where's that lady you call Captain?"

Standing close enough to hear what was transpiring the Captain spoke up and said she was Captain Neal, sir.

"At ease Captain, we're all civilians here. I just wanted to congratulate you on a job well done and if you ever decide you want a civilian job, look me up.``

"Thank you sir but I just did what I was told. It's S and W who should get the credit."

The Lieutenant just laughed and looked at JR and said, "She's a keeper."

Sam who was sitting back relaxing yelled over, "That's what I said. And she even drinks that shitty German beer."

Once everything was loaded up and JR and the Lieutenant had finished talking the group headed home. Everyone's adrenaline had started slowing down and a long day was taking its toll.

The captain who had worked the hardest sat up front in the passenger seat.

After a few minutes of silence the captain asked Barbara if she was a full time driver for S and W..

Explaining she was a detective who worked in Florida and it was an honor to drive these knuckleheads.

The captain asked a few more questions and Barabara answered honestly as she had been asked to do.

The captain knew there was more to this company than she was seeing.

Pulling into home base the house was dark. Rita had made sure to leave a spot empty in the garage so Babara backed in and waited till Rita gave the okay before knocking on the side of the van saying all clear.

The captain grabbed her duffel bag before Barbara told her to leave it. She had everything waiting upstairs in her room.

"I need clothes for tomorrow and something to wear tonight. And shampoo. Lots of shampoo!"

Barabara told her to trust her.

Inside Sam kissed Rita and said he was going to bed, he was tired from solving this case.

Thomas kissed Katie and said they were going to bed.

The Doc and Maggie had retired very soon after the computer was loaded into the van..

GD Dog had followed everyone inside, got a drink of water, growled at JR and went upstairs to join his sister in a warm comfortable bed.

David kissed Tina and said he was hungry. Tina said get a plate to go and they were going to bed.

Michelle had taken Little Sammy and the dogs and was already in bed. Rita showed the Captain where her bedroom was located and as the two came back down said she would clean up everything tomorrow and she followed Sam out to the boat.

JR was hungry. He had barely eaten dinner, worried that he had forgotten something so his stomach overtook his tiredness.

Grabbing a little bit of everything JR sat next to the Captain who looked like she was eating for two.

Eating in silence the Captain finally asked JR exactly what they did.

JR was tired and knew he had to be up early.

"Captain, it's late and I'm tired and I want to go kiss my wife who will pretend she's sleeping but I know her sleeping snore and she 's waiting for me to tell her I love her and kiss her goodnight before she goes to sleep. So I have a proposition for you. Stay with us for a day, two days, three days as long as you like. Relax, hang by the pool, read, go fishing with Sam and us, rent a car, whatever you like and you'll see what S and W is all about. And ask any members of S and W anything. Now I'm going to bed. Breakfast is between 6:30 and 8 if the weather is nice outside in the lanai. Good night Captain. You did a great job and S and W owes you one."

The captain who had worked in numerous operations through out the world with some of the top people in their field could not believe she had just completed one of the most complicred bomb removals in such a short time with everyine involved so relaxed. She could get used to this.

Chapter 13

JR did not not want to get up but he knew today was going to be the day that Mama's Clan was going down. Leaving Michelle sleeping he made his way downstairs.. Sam of course was up and bright eyed and bushy tailed. Going out on the lanai after making a cup of coffee, he was surprised to see Maggie and the Captain up already sitting there next to each other talking like two old friends.

Rita was walking up from the boat and asked JR what the hell he was doing up.

No, no, no. "Get your ass upstairs and you relax a little longer next to your wife. The cameras saw you so we need you refreshed, GD Dog you stay down here, and we're going to make sure you're up by 8. Now go! And take a shower for god's sake before you come back down."

JR didn't argue, but silently went back to bed.

Awoken by GD Dog pounding on his back, JR looked over at the clock and saw it was 8:45. What happened to 8?

Grabbing a quick shower and throwing on a pair of shorts, sandals and some kind of Hawaiian shirt he came downstairs and made another cup of coffee. Coffee in hand he was greeted by the entire gang to applause saying they were so happy he woke up.

Sam asked if he had banker hours,

Thomas wanted to know if he was ready for the nursing home.

Mark just looked at him and said he hoped he never got old.

JR was feeling 100 percent better as he kissed Michelle and Lil Sam and of course GD Dog. He asked what someone needed to do to get breakfast around here.

Sitting down Rita took a seat next to him, JR asked Rita what he missed.

"Let's see. Maggie said she's going to take the job but she's not dealing with explosives, your Captain told everyone to call her Gail and was staying for a couple of days, and if everything goes as planned S and W should clear about $95,000. So after salaries, etcetera were looking at about $35,0000 in the kitty. "Not bad but it should have been better. Our mistake for underestimating them. Those bitches."

"No worries. My gut is telling me you may be able to add an extra zero to that figure."

It appeared as if Rita had everything under control. The guys were starting to unload the van filled with supplies. The stones and blocks were placed as Maggie and the Doc supervised. Tina, Katiie, Laurie and Tim were working on the computer trying to find a backdoor to allow them access plus something to do with that incoming phone sensor.

JR thanked Rita for handling everything.

"Today JR I'm going to request you take it easy. I have Maggie and the Doc working with Laurie's Dad on the ladder scenario, Thomas is going to work with the Lieutenant and I'll be the go between Tina and the folks working with her. We can handle this JR. You got us to this point, let us take it the rest of the way."

"What the hell am I supposed to do?"

"Phil and Barbara will be arriving here soon with the new IT guy, Peter. Tina booked him an earlier flight and he's coming in to help her with the computer. Till lunch and after lunch you and Michelle are going to look at the cases the other teams are working on and give your advice. We also would like for you to go over the budget with Barbara And finally you're going to look at the opening of the North Office and see what we need. And as far as today goes you will be kept in the loop on everything that's going on. Let me say this was a universal decision from all the detectives. Now Phil can explain more but for now you take it easy. After breakfast, why not get in the pool with your wife. You two haven't spent much quality time together these past few days. Oh and one last item, Sam said he picked you to follow in his footsteps and it's your responsibility to find someone to follow in yours. And Sam did say it doesn't have to be a guy."

Rita looked over at the Captain laying on a raft.

JR looked at the Captain and back at Rita.

"Really? You got to be shiten me."

Rita just smiled and said, "It's your decision JR. You never know which road to take until you travel it. And remember, this isn't a decision that has to be made today, tomorrow or even this month. Just think about it."

Phil arrived twenty minutes later followed by a gentleman who reminded JR as a middle aged Harrison Ford but not as tall and with more hair. And he wore glasses. Okay, maybe not Harrison Ford.

Everyone who was outside was introduced to Peter.

Sam, being Sam as usual, asked Peter if he knew how to cook.

Peter looked at Phil who told him to ignore Sam. "He's old and senile. Let's get you inside with Tina and the computer. She will explain where she's at."

"I heard that. I'll show you whose old and senile when I'm cooking your burger tonight. You'll be getting some of the special JR sauce on yours."

Thomas came over to JR and told him that the cell phones will now be legally monitored and traced and that a soft perimeter was in place around the Homosassa location. If any of the ladies showed up they would be held for trespassing. Lieutenant Dan also said to tell you he will be here at two and if there's no cold Margaritas he's not mentioning S and W at all to the press.

Thomas and JR were best of fiends, so JR had no problem asking Thomas what the fuck he was doing voting that JR was supposed to be a what.? A guy in charge of cases? A supervisor?

"Yes JR. It's your destiny. I didn't want to be born a tall good looking intelligent black man who is hung like a racehorse but I was. So suck it up buttercup. You're going to do fine. And JR, stop worrying. Everyone knows it. Just accept it and move on. Nothing is going to change except you're not going to be taking as many chances as last night."

"Last night?"

" Yeah last night. You took too many chances, going back and forth , cutting the paneling off the wall to name a couple. Everyone realized how much you and Michelle do everything and if anything happened to you, Michelle would be a basket case. And vice versa. You two are the soul of S and W. So we're keeping you safe. So man up and be a supervisor. "

Next to show up to talk to JR was Laurie, Tim and Katie.

Laurie was the spokesman. "Hey Barbara, Phil. Glad you're here. First I'm supposed to say that Tina and Peter should have the phone activation switch ready in an hour and now with Peter's help they should have the computer unlocked in two hours. She also sent Casanova down to buy an electrical tester. Not a good one but one of those cheap little junky ones that that discount freight gives out for free when you purchase so much. And as far as us, we were worthless. Those two in there now are talking Lingo and numbers we had no idea what they were saying.. I think they were happy we were leaving."

Sam was trying to scoot away quietly when Rita told him and Thomas to get the extra folding tables out of the garage. "Tim, you and the Doc do a beer run and make sure we don't need any alcohol also. And pick up some of that beer Gail drinks. If she's like Sam, get a couple of cases."

"Wait, that's Thomas and my job. We always do the beer runs." Sam was serious.

Rita wasn't having it. "The last time you and Thomas did a beer run together we didn't see you two for over two hours and had chalk on your hands from a pool cue when you came back.. So Tim, Doc, you two now are in charge of beer runs."

Katie, Thomas's better half remembered that too. "Hey Thomas, before you help Sam with those tables could you please grab me another Margarita? I think all the ladies could use a refill."

Laurie's Dad, the painting contractor, showed up in a long bed double cab pick-up with two middle aged and very skinny guys around noon. Laurie went out to greet them and bring them around back where Laurie introduced Maggie.

Laurie's Dad said hello to everyone and seeing Sam moving tables he couldn't resist saying, "Hey Sam, they finally found a use for you!"

Sam always had a comeback. "Hey Laurie I didn't want to say anything before, but this asshole ain't your dad. Your Dad was a Doctor, not an idiot."

Looking at Maggie he asked where she wanted him to set up. Explaining what was needed he started immediately. Next to arrive was Big Jim and Judy from the roofing company the first husband had worked for. Maggie introduced the two owners and being Florida Contractors the two worked together getting set up. In less than five minutes the two were gossiping like two old women. Judy had gone inside the lanai and introduced herself and Michelle was running to get her a bathing suit saying Sam was busy but he'd make her the best Margarita she ever had.

Watching Maggie sweat, JR couldn't take it anymore and told Maggie she could supervise from underneath an umbrella with a fan blowing on her as well as out in the sun.

The guys had the ladder up when Maggie came out of the lanai and showed the guys the picture. "Now right now is where the ladder should have been set up. Jim swears he never would have put the feet so close to an edge where it was found."

Asking one of the workers to help her move it she placed it close to the edge.

"What everyone seems to believe is that Ryan placed this foot of the ladder here and it slipped and ended up in the soft dirt causing the ladder to tilt to the right and because he was carrying a five gallon bucket the momentum caused the ladder with Ryan on it where he fell and broke bones on the right side of his body but the fatal blow was when he hit the block here with his head. Now there were vague markings on the concrete where it appeared that what they say was true but were things anyone who had practiced this would have known and brought something with them to create those marks, And were sure the person who did this was not seen by Ryan or he would have been more cautious. We think"

JR got a call from Lieutenant Dan saying Sandra was on her way.

" Who called her?"

"The mother. She called and told her that it was a beautiful day and all the bees were so busy it would be a good time for a drive to the country. And the bitch was laughing as she said it."

"Perfect. Are you still sticking with the plan?"

" Of course. It's a good plan."

JR looked at Phil and called Thomas and Sam over and told them Sandra was on her way. "And what's even funnier is Mom called her and told her to do it. And she was laughing when she told her."

Phil asked JR how long was he going to keep the ladder charade up?

"Until someone figures it out or 45 minutes"

Fifteen minutes later Maggie looked at the picture again. What she saw was a coiled up garden hose next to the house. Why hadn't she noticed that before.

"Michelle, Tina's busy so could you take this picture and blow it up where the garden hose is sitting?"

Taking a pen from Phil she drew a square on the picture that she needed blown up.

Coming back a few minutes later Michelle handed her the close up.

Studying the picture Maggie turned and looked at JR who told Maggie, "I was thinking about it. Now go prove it. There's a garden hose right over there you can use."

Making the Doc help her she unhooked the garden hose and looking at the picture placed it to the right of the ladder and next to the house. She stood looking at the hose and then the ladder. Grabbing the hose nozzle she placed the squeeze handle on one side of the right hand ladder side and the male part on the other side of the strut. Walking ten feet she pulled as hard as she could. The ladder came down exactly as she thought it would. Now she needed proof.

"Okay who's the victim?"

Laurie's Dad had brought harnesses and plenty of rope. The oldest and skinniest of the two workers volunteered. Setting up the harnesses and ropes the two contractors double and triple checked everything. Climbing the ladder with a five gallon bucket was hard enough. Carrying a full 5 gallon bucket was harder than hell.

Jim told those around him that there was no way Ryan would have taken all those tools and caulk up. Someone added some things while he was laying there." That was a new twist that JR hadn't thought of.

Arriving at the roof edge the worker placed the bucket on the roof and slid it forward as he came off the ladder onto the roof.

Jim yelled up and told him to come down now.
The worker was struggling with the five gallon bucket due to its weight. Told to remove everything but 4 tubes of caulking, the caulk gun and a utility scraper and throw the rest down on the ground the worker was able to start down easily. Once he was just past the reach of the roof Maggie told him to hold on and that she was going to pull. And pull she did, watching as the ladder fell exactly as she had hoped. Of course the man who had volunteered was caught by the harnesses before he hit the ground

A round of applause greeted Maggie and you would have thought she found the cure for cancer. Doc was beaming like a proud father. Setting the ladder back up to retrieve the man suspended there JR called Tim over. "Could you ask Maggie to do it one more time and videotape it this time please?"

Telling Maggie, JR watched as she turned to him and slowly raised her middle finger. Turning back to the guys she said she needed to video tape it and she was offering the guy who was just getting on the ladder an additional $100.00 to do it one more time.. And since she was video taping she would need a volunteer to pull the hose.

JR was waiting for a status on the computer when Rita, Tina and Peter came out. He could tell it was good news by their expressions.

"We have good news and bad news. First the good news. We got into the computer and we have everything printing out right now. And when I say everything I mean everything. Your going to have a fucking novel when its done printing."

JR knew they had enough for Mom and two of the sisters but his worry was Julie.

" Please tell me you got something on Julie?"

" That's the bad news. It appears as if Julie's name is never mentioned or at least so far."

Shit that was the worst news he could have received. Calling Thomas and Sam over again he discussed what he thought they should do. Both of them agreed.

Picking up his cell phone he called Lieutenant Dan.

"Hey, it's JR. I don't have time to explain but we need to pick up Kristen immediately and she can't use any phone. Let Sandra start to go inside the trailer but grab her before she can open the entry door. And again, no phone. And their lawyer. That son of a bitch knows a lot more than he's saying I'm betting. Pick him up on some bogus arrest if you have to. Speeding tickets whatever but again no phone. The mother is going to be leaving Julie's house very soon. We need you to pick her up and the same thing goes. No phone. You do that and we will give you all the credit and a big donation to the charity of your choosing now please make us proud. It is very important they do not use any phone. Got it? Okay call me when they're under lock and key and I'll give you the next step.

Chapter 14

Time went by slowly. A minute felt like an hour as everyone waited.

The Lieutenant finally called. "All three, including the lawyer, are as snug as a bug in a rug."

JR had been waiting patiently for the call. "I don't have time to make fun of you saying that right now. Now you may want to write this next part down. You're going to bring Sandra into the interrogation room and tell her that they have her for trespassing so far. We're having a hard time figuring out whose property it is and since you won't tell us we brought the K-9s in. We're not sure what's going on unless you want to tell us, She won't. You continue: Okay, you have 30 minutes before the swat team gets there and starts going through the house and trust me they're good. You have any drugs, weapons or explosives your fucked. Now I'm going to ask you one more time, ``What were you doing there?" She still won't answer and she'll say she wants her lawyer. At that point let her make a call. I'm betting she first calls her mother. Then Kristen and finally she will call the family lawyer who is unable to answer. If she has his number. Finally as a last resort she'll call Julie and that's what we want. Julie is the brains and was smart enough to keep her name out of everything. And I'm betting she's the only one with the code. We need Julie to call the phone device on the computer. I'm betting one of the three family members, including Mom will break when their charged with murder and have to give up the money and property they received. And Dan, let her wait in between calls. The longer she has to wait the more nervous she's going to become. We want her to be good and scared before she calls Julie. And keep reminding her of the time before the Swat team gets to the trailer.

"Damn JR, that's good and it just might work amazingly. Did Michelle think of this? Come on, be honest."

"Just do this. We're getting tired of this fucking case.. We're going to go ahead and record the computer device when Julie activates it. You'll have a live feed going to your base computer and in the police station in Homosassa. computer. Give me a quick call when Sandra talks to Julie and we'll start the live feed. Wait, you have that pen still? Write down this number for Thomas who's going to be handling this from now on. You've met him playing cards and he's a good guy. Thanks Dan. Oh one last thing, I'm sure you realize this but don't let anyone go inside that trailer until the bomb squad has gone through it. Call Thomas on his number and have our Captain talk to them first. We think you may have more hidden explosives in the bathroom doorway and probably a few other surprises. She'll explain it to them.``

Finishing the call Thomas looked at JR and asked him exactly what he was supposed to do.

"Don't ask me. This is your case now. If it was me I'd have a meeting with everyone and ask them. Good Luck. If you do feel that you need advice, come to me anytime. Apparently that's my new job. You voted for it. Think of it as your destiny."

Thomas looked at JR and said that he was even taking his destiny line?

JR just laughed and laughed even harder when Thomas said he was going to tell Lil Sam what an asshole his father was.

"Suck it up buttercup."

The call to Julie went exactly as JR had hoped it would. Having tried to reach anyone Sandra was desperate by the time she called Julie.

Answering the phone Julie knew it had to be one of the three since the caller ID said police.

"Julie, it's Sandra. They got me for trespassing at a country house. In less than 10 minutes Swat is bringing in a team. They think there might be explosives inside. A dog alerted them to it. We need to do it now. Julie, please do it now. I can take the heat for trespassing but the other is a big no. Help us Julie, you have to do it now. We helped you now help us."

Julie was calm and collected. "Sandra, don't worry. We'll get you a good lawyer and get the trespassing charges dropped. As for the other, it will be gone so no worries there. Just relax and don't say a word."

It was a good five minutes later that the cheap electrical meter registered more than enough voltage to set the plastic explosives off. The call of course came from Julie's house number.

JR was smiling. "Okay, wait for it."

The electrical meter went dead. Ten seconds later it came back on. This happened one more time before it stopped.

JR, still smiling, looked at everyone and said, "Well Julie now know's we have the computer."

The day had finally come when she knew she would have to face the consequences of her deeds. She had tried to accomplish her life long goal of killing for monetary gain and she had failed. She had at least tried. Watching everyday as panhandlers held their cardboard signs asking for money as they stood next to a sign in a business that read 'Help wanted' or as everyday people went to a job they hated while barely making ends meet, she had at least given it her all to become wealthy and had not played by the so called 'rules of the land'.

She knew that when they had begun that Kristen's ideal of using her bitch girlfriend Maria was not a perfect plan. Too many loose ends. Looking back she knew that she should have just said 'Fuck this' and waited. But after years and not being found out she even thought to herself that the government was really that stupid and it was perfect. She realized now she should have just gone ahead and blown up the trailer but she hesitated. She was so sure setting up S and W to make fools of themselves and suing the insurance company would work. She had underestimated them and they had in turn played her like a fool. This morning when her mother and her watched as they were setting up the ladder scenario they laughed thinking S and W had no idea what they were doing. She knew now that it was S and W who was laughing at them.

When she had called three times and the phone activation switch still rang she knew they had the computer and it would show the number was coming from this house. The police she knew were on their way here. There was no way out but one.

As she fixed her tea she thought to herself that she had gotten so very close that she had started seeing the light at the end of the tunnel. But that was not to be. Like death you could not decide on the time or day or year of when fate would screw you over. When your fucked your fucked. But at least she could choose her own time and day of death. She smiled to herself as she left a note and drank a nice hot cup of relaxing tea.

It was 20 minutes later that Lieutenant Dan called Tim and said Julie had committed suicide by drinking a very relaxing, very strong cup of tea. "She also left a note. It was addressed To Maggie and S and W. It read: ' Fuck you. Hugs and kisses. Nice job. See you on the other side ass holes. Julie.' The guys at the station thought it was very touching,"

As Thomas told everyone a sigh of relief passed through the detectives.

"Any obstacles?" JR asked.

"The Leautenant told me they had a bomb tech go in first and basically walked right in. There was nothing. Seeing how the trailer was rigged I'm kind of surprised."

JR wasn't. "What you have to realize is though the ladies were killer's they weren't killing for pleasure. They only killed if there was money in it. Julie knew she had failed and I'm thinking the thought of going to jail was not in her plans and probably scared her more then death. What did he say about the trailer?"

I asked and he said he would be here in an hour and he was bringing Julie's personal computer with him. He also said don't forget about the pitcher of Margaritas."

JR asked Michelle if she needed a break from reviewing the cases. Saying no he looked at Barbara and Phil who also said they were fine.

Rita knew JR and knew it was killing him just sitting there. "You know Phil, I think we can finish this up tomorrow but has anyone decided on the Captain? I think JR should talk to her about working for us. And where's Sam?

Thomas had grabbed a cold beer and was sitting close with Katie who was taking a break from the pool. "Sam and Big Jim are on your boat. Turns out Big Jim is also an avid fisherman. He's showing Sam had to use that new fish finder. Big Jim knows he's going to be coming into some money that he was sued for so he's happier than a pig in shit. "

Katie told Thomas he was spending way too much time with Sam. He was even starting to talk like him.

JR wanted to know why Thomas wasn't down there with them cause you know Sam's going to forget half of what he's telling him. JR knew that Thomas was waiting in case Lieutenant Dan called. Telling Thomas he had a cell phone and if he didn't go they would have to listen to Sam bitch about there must be something wrong with the damn thing the next time they went fishing.

Michelle told JR that she had already talked to Gail regarding a position here at S and W. "When I told her what it paid she didn't hesitate plus for some unknown reason she likes the people here. She did say she wanted to stay in Florida. And it also turns out that Maggie is leaning more towards staying in Florida. I think she likes our company.

JR just looked at Rita.

"It's your call JR."

"Katie? Let me guess. You and Thomas want to stay too?"

Katie as always took a minute before answering. "Thomas would never admit it but he loves Sam and you like brothers and he'd probably be wishing he was down here fishing and partying and missing everyone if he was up north. And I would too. You folks are the dysfunctional family I never had."

"All right then. That just leaves Peter. Let me call Tina."

Calling Tina he asked her to ask Peter if he had any problems working here in Florida if they offered him a job.

" He said not in the least as long as he gets two new computers, a new chair and he wants two weeks vacation and moving expenses."

"You didn't tell him anything about S and W and the pay and benefits?"

"No. I wanted to make sure you were going to hire him first."

"Yes, we are offering him a detective position so go ahead. I have a feeling Peters is going to be a very happy detective. And with the kind of money he's going to be making he can buy his own damn chair. We will get him two new computers. Barbara, can you please get with Tim and have him order them? And check with Tina too. "

JR told everyone that was it till Lieutenant Dan left and then they would have a meeting afterwards. He also asked Phil to get the paperwork ready for three new detectives and have them sign it before the Lieutenant got here.

Lieutenant Dan arrived 30 minutes later carrying a computer which Tim took from him to give to Tina. Everyone was waiting for what he had to say.

Doctor D had made not one but three pitchers of Margaritas and Sam had also convinced the Doc to cook dinner that night. Told him he overheard Maggie saying to Rita how she thought it was so sexy when he cooked.

Everyone was waiting like little kids getting ready to hear someone tell 'The Night Before Christmas' book on Christmas Eve. Lieutenant Dan who was drinking a Margarita and had taken his shoes off and started by telling everyone that S and W really knew how to handle a case. "And by the way, not that anyone cares you can now call me Captain Dan. Turns out by supervising Mr. Wood's detectives from your Insurance Agency Maggie and making you video tape everything and handling the suspects in the way I did, I was just informed my ass is moving up the ladder."

Maggie was confused. Just when she was getting a handle on everything something always came up to throw her for a loop.

"There won't be anything mentioned about S and W but everyone from officers up to the Mayor knows it was S and W, again."

It was Rita who gave a big thanks to the newly promoted Lieutenant.

"Now JR you folks were right on everything. There were alot more hidden surprises in there and they're still working on clearing it. And thank you Captain for your help. The job offer still stands."

The Captain thanked him but told him she had already accepted a job with S and W.

"Smart woman. I wish they had offered me a job but they realized I would end up shooting Sam."

The Captain thought to herself that there was more going on with Lieutenant Dan than was being told.

"So as of a few minutes ago all the ladies are being charged with murder for Julie's two deceased husband's, storing explosives with the the intent to harm, check forging and a few other major charges. Those ladies are going to jail for a long time. As soon as the bomb techs give the all clear the Detectives are standing by to take fingerprints off everything. I want to ask Tina a quick question. What did you find on the data coming out of the computer? Did Michelle get a chance to read it yet?"

"Damn Lieutenant, we just printed it out and so no she hasn't had time to read it. We're making a copy of everything for you to take with you but I can tell you this : It contains everything from purchasing and making plastic explosives to learning about propane tanks to what they ordered on Amazon and Walmart and a few places in China. And they did research on S and W. So you give this copy to the prosecutors and they will have no problem making a case. And one last item of importance: the gentleman to my right is Peter. You can get with Phil and get his new cell phone number. Mark on I will be leaving the day after tomorrow for a tropical island vacation for a few days and Peter will be taking my spot. We would leave tomorrow but I'm giving someone a chance to go shopping and buy me a fucking engagement ring which I thought he would do when he was gone for two weeks. And we better not get any fucking phone calls or surprises while we're away. And yes I'm talking to you Sam, JR and Thomas. You do anything to ruin or mess with us while we're gone. I will come back and I swear I'll cut your balls off."

Rita was almost laughing, "Very nicely said Tina. I especially like the part about cutting their balls off. And I'm sure that any man who would be stupid enough to do anything like that would probably not mind sleeping on the couch for a month, and that goes for the Doc, Tim and you to Phil. I know you guys. Go ahead Lieutenant Dan."

"We'll let me be the first to congratulate you two on your upcoming engagement and I wish you the best, especially you Mark. So getting back to the case, Sandra, once she heard Julie had committed suicide ask for a state apointed lawyer. So did Kristen. And the mother. No one has talked yet but I'm betting it's Sandra."

JR asked Lieutenant Dan how much he was willing to bet?

"I got ten dollars."

"You're going to lose it. Right now or very soon Mom's going to take a plea if she admits what really happened. Her version will be that it was all Julie and that she was scared to death of her daughter. It was Julie that pulled the ladder out from underneath Ryan and it was Julie that blew up the second husband. She knew about but was so afraid for her life she had to remain silent or Julie would kill her too.

But to be honest with you, I really don't give a shit anymore. We proved that it was murder and one way or another Sandra, Kristen and Mom will get their just reward. Now unless your chief wants anymore help on this case he will need to go through Phil and work out payment. As of now S and W have done what we are being paid to do. We proved that these weren't accidents for our clients. Now Dan, we're done and your help has been tremendous and we couldn't have done it without you. But starting tomorrow S and W are going to be looking at new cases we have waiting for us and after a few days of R and R we are going back to the grind. Right now I'm going to take GD Dog for a walk and afterwards give him a much needed B-A-T-H. Then I'm grabbing an ice cold beer and spend some time with my wife in the pool and then having a nice dinner with my friends here. We will talk during dinner about S and W and I'll explain everything to our new detectives. But for now we are officially done with this case."

No one asked any more questions. The case was over just like that. Everyone acted as if the past three days never happened.

As JR was walking out the side door with GD Dog, Maggie asked if she could join him.

JR knew she had questions. Walking just a little ways Maggie asked JR if all the cases were like this one.

"You mean over?"

"Ha Ha. I mean we just walk away? Shouldn't we have more research or something to find out if we missed something? It just seems like we are walking away from this case with a lot more to be discovered."

"Not going to happen. Maggie we got paid to do a job which was to prove if these may be accidents or murder. We did it. We will get paid and move on. It's now up to the State Agencies to take it from here. I told you S and W had two rules: Enjoy life and family and make money. That's our goal. And right now you should be enjoying life with Doc talking about moving down here, which I now understand you would like to do. And I'm thrilled to have both of you working here. You're going to be fine if you follow those two rules."

JR could tell Maggie was still confused. "Maggie, most people whether they realize it or not, will try and get anything extra they can. Before I went into the military I worked in construction and maintenance. I'd be sent out to paint a door and 50% of the owners would say to me 'since you have the paint out would you mind touching this up? ' The people don't even realize they're doing it. Now we could spend another week or so digging up facts but for whose benefits? Not ours. Next question.'"

"Why are you allowing my insurance company and the police to take all the credit? I would think you want some big time advertising saying S and W solved a case no one else could?"

"Maggie, in every contract Phil sends out is a clause stating that S and W is to have little or no publicity and that the signee is responsible to ensuring that with the help from S and W, Now with your company it was easy, it makes it look that their on their toes and keeps insurance rates down because they pursue customers who try and take advantage of them Mr. Gants and Mr. Woods' accounts are going to increase big time. And it will make the people who want to screw over their companies think twice. For them it's a win-win situation. Now just stop and think. What would happen to S and W in this case, which I wouldn't be surprised went nationwide, if we did that? I'll tell you. We would have reporters out of our ass climbing on top of each other to get an interview with anyone from S and W. . They would be outside our house. And our phone wouldn't stop ringing. Not just from reporters but from desperate people wanting S and W to solve a missing case or a murder or countless other crimes no one can solve. Think about it and you'll see I'm right. "

 Maggie said she had one more question if JR didn't mind.

"Maggie you can ask anything you want to anybody at S and W and we will answer you. That's what being a detective is all about."

"All right. What the hell did you hire me for? What am I supposed to do for S and W to benefit this company? I'm an older, short white woman whose joints hurt in the morning. I get drunk after two beers and I hate fishing and can hardly figure out how to use my remote control; on my television and don't even ask me about my DVD player. So why me?"

JR actually did laugh. GD Dog turned around to look at what was so funny.

"Maggie you have been stuck in a job for years that though you may have enjoyed, offered very little use of your brain. Could you ever go back and look at an insurance claim again after going through the investigation and not thinking this person is lying? You can't. And in a couple of years you'll be able to distinguish who's lying and who's not. And like this case, sometimes it's just luck and sometimes it's just fate. We can't choose what life has in store for us, what we can choose is to work hard and enjoy life. Trust me Maggie, a whole new world is about to be opened to you. And everyone at S and W agrees. You have what it takes."

As she was taking her last few breaths of life she smiled and thought to herself of what could have been. She knew that she was smarter than those peons at S and W. They had thought they had won and were laughing at her still. Oh, if they only knew the surprises in store for them even in her death.

Chapter 15   Eight Months Later

Sitting by Michelle on the lanai and holding their new daughter,
JR could not be happier. GD Dog was by his side thinking great, another pup in the house.
Venus dog was laying by Little Sam thinking how she was going to protect Lil Sam and this
new one called Gail?
Thinking back he remembered how he never knew happiness until he had found
Michelle. Now with two wonderful children and two somewhat abnormal dogs he could
not ask for anything more in life.
It was then that GD Dog sat up and let out a soft whine. JR bent slightly to scratch GD
Dog's ears thinking GD Dog had a bad dream.
The first bullet hit him in his shoulder, the second on his chest missing his heart by just
fractions of an inch the third bullet as he slump over grazed his back.

As someone had once written: You can't control fate.

Another person had said to enjoy each day as if it was your last. You only live once.

____

Join us December 2022 for Book Four in the series 'Chances are'.

www.ingramcontent.com/pod-product-compliance
Lightning Source LLC
Chambersburg PA
CBHW031354160726
47993CB00002B/967